GODDESS'S HOPE

THE CHILDREN OF THE GODS ORIGINS BOOK 2

I. T. LUCAS

Also by I. T. Lucas

SETS

THE CHILDREN OF THE GODS BOOKS 1-3: DARK STRANGER TRILOGY—INCLUDES A BONUS SHORT STORY: **THE FATES TAKE A VACATION**

THE CHILDREN OF THE GODS: BOOKS 1-6—INCLUDES CHARACTER LISTS

THE CHILDREN OF THE GODS: BOOKS 6.5-10 —INCLUDES CHARACTER LISTS

TRY THE CHILDREN OF THE GODS SERIES ON **AUDIBLE**

2 FREE audiobooks with your new Audible subscription!

NAVUH

*A*s the servants opened the double doors to the throne room, Mortdh strode in with his usual confident swagger.

Walking a few paces behind him, Navuh did the same—his head held high and his shoulders squared. As Mortdh's official successor, he expected to be received with all the fanfare and respect due to a god, regardless of his mixed blood.

Unlike his father, though, who focused exclusively on his arch nemesis, Navuh took a quick stock of everyone in the room.

Up on the dais, Ahn sat on his throne with his mate on one side and his daughter on the other. Both were beautiful and regal, but where the mother's expression was perfectly schooled to conceal her emotions, Annani's eyes blazed with contempt for her spurned intended.

No amount of gifts was going to change the little spitfire's mind and convince her to mate Mortdh. Their only hope was in persuading Ahn to fulfil his promise and force Annani into the prearranged joining.

As a leader, Ahn should realize that his daughter's happiness was inconsequential considering what was at stake—a bloody war that would further reduce the gods' tiny population.

Not that it was a bad outcome necessarily.

In Navuh's opinion, the arrogant super-beings had outlived their usefulness, and it was time for their progeny to rule. With immortals outnumbering gods in the thousands and almost as powerful, they should take the lead.

Or rather Navuh should.

But he was not ready yet. There was still much to be learned, and building an army of warriors who were loyal to him and not his father was a complicated endeavor that could not be rushed.

Navuh stifled a smirk.

He had convinced Mortdh that in order to win against the other gods, their army of immortal warriors had to be able to block the gods' brain manipulation—the only advantage gods had over immortals. What Mortdh had not figured out, however, was that those immortal warriors would be able to keep him out as well.

It was not easy, and not all warriors could do that even with proper training, but in a century or so Navuh would amass enough of those who could.

And that was why his father had to mate Annani.

With Mortdh temporarily satisfied, he would not feel the need to strike out right away.

Hopefully.

His father's ambition to rule over all the gods burned hot. He would either get the throne legitimately by mating Annani and waiting patiently for Ahn to step down, or he would take it by force.

As it was, keeping Mortdh's internal volcano of rage from erupting was taxing Navuh's diplomatic capabilities to the max. His father was insane, but he was also brilliant and highly suspicious. Managing him was becoming more and more difficult.

If Ahn did not fulfill his promise to Mortdh, the results would be catastrophic, and not only for Navuh's clandestine plans.

With their army not ready for war yet, his insane father might consider using unconventional means. Navuh did not know what those means were, but Mortdh had seemed exceedingly smug when talking about his 'secret weapon.'

Ahn rose to his feet and descended the three steps from the dais. Spreading his arms, he met Mortdh and Navuh in the middle of the throne room. "Welcome, nephew. It is so good of you to visit." He offered Mortdh a big fake smile before embracing him and clapping him on his back.

"Thank you, uncle, for welcoming my son and me into your home." Mortdh motioned for Navuh to come closer.

Navuh bowed. "It is an honor."

As Ahn returned to his throne, Mortdh and Navuh took their seats in front of the dais.

"May I proceed directly to the reason for my visit?" Mortdh asked.

Navuh stifled a groan. His father was not much of a diplomat.

Navuh would have spent several long minutes on pleasantries before getting to the point, buttering Ahn up and making him more receptive to his plea.

Antagonizing the leader was the last thing Mortdh should be doing.

Not that it mattered. Ahn did not seem perturbed. "Please, speak freely, nephew. We are family. We can dispense with unnecessary chitchat."

"Apparently, the princess believes she has found her fated truelove, but I beg to differ. Annani is still very young and impressionable. She has fallen into the clutches of a usurper."

Great. Mortdh had just managed to offend both Ahn and Annani.

Ahn lifted a brow. "Do you not trust me to ensure the virtue of a contender for my daughter's hand?"

Mortdh bowed his head in mock respect. "Naturally, my lord. But you are too busy with the affairs of state to pay close attention to your daughter." He lifted his hand in the sign for peace. "I am guilty of the same. I should have paid better attention to my precious intended. In my defense, I have waited for her to reach the age of majority before coming to court her as a young woman, and not a child. But just like you, my lord, I have been preoccupied with affairs of state and waited too long. I am here to rectify my negligence."

Navuh exhaled a relieved breath. That was much better. Taking a share of the blame was a smart move.

"Please have my lovely intended's gifts brought in." Mortdh waved a hand.

Navuh pushed to his feet and bowed. "Of course, Father."

As the guards opened the doors, Navuh signaled for the servants waiting outside to enter. Lifting their overflowing baskets, they formed a line as he had instructed them to.

The last were the slaves that had been captured up north—savage humans who were so primitive they were just a step above apes. What made them unique, though, was their pallidity. The lack of direct sunlight in their corner of the world must have reduced their pigmentation in the same way the nearly complete darkness of the gods' home world had done to the gods.

Mortdh thought that the combination made them exotic. Navuh did not share his father's opinion. The northerners were good for nothing other than digging trenches. They would not make good palace servants. Therefore, they were useless to the princess.

As they had been instructed, the savages immediately dropped to the floor in deep obeisance.

"Who are these people?" Annani asked in a haughty tone.

Mortdh puffed up his chest. "Exotic slaves captured in the north."

Annani's temper flared, and she spat out, "Slaves? You brought me slaves as gifts?"

Ahn shushed her with a quick wave of his hand. "Did all these people sell themselves into slavery, Mortdh?"

"No, but these are savages, my lord. They hardly qualify as people. They are nomads who hunt for their sustenance. It is like capturing a herd of wild horses. You would not ask a horse if it wants to serve, would you?"

"I would not say that primitive people who lack culture are equivalent to horses. But I will let it slide this time. In the future, though, you should adhere to the law, nephew. After all, without laws we are no better than these savages, am I right?"

Mortdh inclined his head. "I thought the princess would be awed by creatures never seen before in these parts."

"I am sure she is. Annani is very inquisitive. She would love to learn about the northern lands from these people. Please have them escorted out. My servants will provide them with a meal."

Mortdh signaled for Navuh to let the savages and the servants out of the throne room.

"My dear nephew," Ahn said as the room emptied. "I appreciate the effort you have put into trying to convince Annani to accept you, but I am afraid the Fates have made up their minds and chosen another for her. I, for one, do not want to tangle with them lest they retaliate, and neither should you."

Mortdh made a move to stand, but Ahn lifted a hand. "Hear me out, nephew. I think I have a solution that will be satisfactory to all parties involved. From the start, this joining was about politics and not love, a way for us to solidify our ties. We can still have that. I can no longer give you my daughter Annani, but I can give you my other daughter, Areana."

Areana?

Upon hearing Ahn's shocking announcement, Navuh barely managed to remain seated and school his expression into an indifferent mask.

Ahn was offering sweet Areana to Mortdh? Was he out of his mind?

Not only was she the gentlest of souls—the least suitable mate for a male like Mortdh—she was also a widow who was still mourning the loss of her truelove.

Their leader was indeed just as heartless and as ruthless as Mortdh had asserted. Had he no feelings for his own flesh and blood?

What had those two innocent women done to deserve this?

Had they plotted their father's demise much in the same way Navuh had been plotting his?

Unlikely.

First of all, Ahn treated Annani's mother with respect bordering on reverence, so other than his promise to Mortdh, the princess had no reason to resent her father. Besides, she was too young for plotting.

And as for Areana, she was just too sweet and gentle to wish anyone harm, even the father who had ignored her for most of her life, acting as if he was ashamed of her.

At least the little redhead had enough spunk and willpower to stand up to Mortdh. Her sister, on the other hand, was a true sacrificial lamb. His father was going to ruin whatever was left of her spirit.

But not if Navuh could help it.

For decades, he had admired the beautiful, gentle goddess from afar, knowing that as an immortal he was beneath her, and that Areana would never consider anyone other than a pure-blooded god as a suitable mate.

Not that she had allowed any males to get near after her truelove's death. Not even gods. In time, however, he had hoped that she would get over her grief and seek male companionship.

His.

Navuh was willing to wait, and he had not been waiting idly either.

As Mortdh's official successor, his position was akin to that of a prince, especially if and when his father ascended to the throne. And if that was not enough to make Navuh's mixed blood irrelevant, it would surely not matter when his long-term plans came to fruition, and he became the ruler of gods and immortals alike.

Ahn got up, walked toward the partition, and offered his hand to his daughter. "I present the lovely Areana." He led her down the stairs.

She was just as beautiful as Navuh had remembered—her pale face framed by even paler hair, her pink lips lush, her long lashes fanning over big blue eyes that were full of sadness as well as compassion.

The poor thing was trembling all over. Navuh had a feeling that without Ahn's hand holding her up, Areana's knees would have given way.

Unexpectedly, she lifted her face and looked at him, not

his father, wresting a soft gasp from his throat. Did he imagine the plea for help in those big sad eyes?

"A widow," Mortdh hissed. "Used goods."

As Areana blushed and lowered her head, a sudden calm washed over Navuh. His father's rude comment had managed to do what the countless insults he had hurled at Navuh had not.

He was going to kill the arrogant jerk sooner rather than later and rid the world of the most volatile and dangerous being to threaten its survival in thousands of years.

Before, the dubious title used to belong to Ahn—perhaps not the volatility, but certainly the cruelty and the disregard for human life. Except, after mating Nai, their ruler had mellowed out, and most of the gods had conveniently forgotten what he had done in the past. Contrary to what most immortals and humans were led to believe, Ahn was far from the benevolent leader he pretended to be.

Ignoring Mortdh's rude comment, Ahn went on. "Areana is my daughter and second in line to the throne. What is more, she agrees to the joining. It can be done today if you so wish."

Navuh sucked in a sharp breath, then quickly masked his involuntary response with an indignant sneer.

Mortdh barely spared Areana a glance. "She is pretty, I will admit that. But you need to sweeten the deal. I am getting the short end of the stick here, and I do not like it. You promised me Annani, the first in line to the throne, not the second, and at the time an untouched virgin, not a used woman."

With a nod, Ahn led the trembling Areana back up to the dais and helped her to a chair that had been placed next to Annani.

Taking one last furtive glance at the shaken goddess, Navuh forced his attention back to her father.

"I had a feeling that would be your sentiment, nephew, and I came up with a plan that should be most satisfactory to you. Come, join me at the table."

Ahn stepped down and walked over to the table. He waited for Navuh and Mortdh to join him, and then unfurled a scroll. "Here is my territory." Ahn pointed to the area between the two rivers. "And here is yours." He pointed to Mortdh's northern stronghold.

"As it is," Ahn continued, "There is hardly any contact between the two regions. I am offering you sovereignty over yours. Not complete, you will still need to abide by our laws, but you can be a king of your own territory. Instead of your being subject to my rule, we will form a sort of federation. If any of the gods decide to join you, they will be subject to your rule."

Mortdh rubbed his hand over his new beard—just another thing he had to do differently from all the other gods. Too beautiful to hide their faces behind facial hair, male gods and most immortals kept their faces clean-shaven, but, naturally, the despot had to distinguish himself and those under his rule in every way. Unless Mortdh grew tired of the beard, it would not be long before he passed a decree that all males residing in his territory were forbidden to shave.

His father's vanity knew no bounds.

"An interesting proposition," Mortdh said. "But how does it differ from what is already going on?"

"It makes it legal. You seek acknowledgment and royal succession, right? Now you have it. My line will continue through Annani and her offspring, and yours will continue through Areana and hers." Ahn threaded the fingers of his hands. "Two intertwined monarchies. Instead of having to wait thousands of years for me to step down, you can be king tomorrow. With my congratulations."

It was a very generous proposal, but Navuh doubted Mortdh would agree to it. His father's ambition was to rule over the entire civilized world, not just one part of it.

"Is my proposition satisfactory to you, nephew?"

Mortdh nodded. "I am claiming this entire region." He circled his finger over a much larger territory than what was currently under his control.

"Deal." Ahn offered his hand.

AREANA

"*I* present the lovely Areana." Her sire took her hand and led her down the stairs.

Areana had thought she was ready, but at the last moment, her courage had deserted her.

Mortdh was just too scary. If he had smiled at her, or at least gazed upon her with appreciation, she could have taken comfort in that. Instead, he had looked at her as if she was a piece of dung stuck to the sole of his sandal.

This was such a bad idea.

She should have never agreed to take Annani's place as Mortdh's mate. He obviously did not want her.

The little confidence Areana had concerning her looks had apparently been misguided. Her beauty was nothing like that of Annani. It was like comparing milk to fire. With her flaming red hair and perfect features, her much younger sister was stunningly beautiful. Even her skin glowed brighter. There was nothing subdued about Annani, not her looks and not her spirit.

No wonder Mortdh was disappointed.

Who would want the mousy Areana with her paltry powers instead of the fiery and powerful Annani?

Except, a quick glance at Navuh had given her a small measure of comfort. What she saw in his eyes was what she had hoped to see in Mortdh's.

It was not the first time she had noticed him looking at her with longing.

Navuh had been only a boy when Areana had lost Ahnon, but even then his eyes had shone with cunning intelligence and inner strength. That was why she had noticed him even though she had hardly paid attention to the many immortal children the gods' liaisons with humans had produced.

As he grew up, Navuh had proven that she had been right about him. For an immortal, he was rumored to be incredibly powerful, more so than some of the weaker gods like her. A few years back, Mortdh had officially announced Navuh as his successor.

Still, despite his power and his lofty position, Navuh was not a god and did not look like one. Although his features were just as perfect, his complexion was dark and his hair even darker. Black and glossy, it was pulled back away from his angular face, the long strands tied at his nape.

He looked exotic, even a little dangerous.

Areana found him quite attractive, but she was not interested in male companionship, godly or immortal. Before agreeing to mate Mortdh, she had planned on living her life as a widow and helping out other women who had lost their husbands. There were many of them among the human population, and they needed her help.

It was important work, and Areana felt that she was destined for it.

Otherwise, why would the Fates gift her with a truelove mate only to snatch him away?

"A widow," Mortdh hissed. "Used goods."

Her face heating up, she looked down at her toes to hold back the tears.

Dear Fates, she should have never agreed to her father's request.

The thing was, throughout her life Ahn had barely acknowledged Areana, treating her as an embarrassment that he wanted as far away from himself as possible. So when he had asked her to mate Mortdh and spy for him, Areana's need to finally gain his approval had overshadowed all other considerations. For the first time in her life, her father saw her as an asset and not a liability.

Areana had felt valuable.

Accepting the proposal had earned her Ahn's coveted approval. But perhaps the price of that moment of satisfaction was too high.

As Ahn led her back up the dais and helped her to a chair, Areana's uncontrollable shaking intensified. Holding back the tears was all she could manage to save her dignity.

The rest of the meeting had gone by in a blur. She would have not survived it without Annani's warm hand on her cold one providing silent support.

"You do not have to do it," Annani whispered as soon as the doors closed behind Mortdh and Navuh.

Fates, how she wished it were true. But it was too late to decline an offer she had already accepted. "I have given my word. I cannot back down now."

Pulling on her hand, Annani helped her up. "Come, let us talk some more in my room."

"Are you sure it is okay?"

"Of course. You are my half-sister."

With a quick glance at Nai, who nodded her approval, Areana let Annani lead her out of the throne room.

Behind them, several maids and guards followed. Areana wondered how many would accompany them into Annani's rooms. For sure the princess's personal maids would be allowed inside, and maids gossiped, which meant no privacy.

Except, Annani did not let anyone into her private chambers. "I want to have a talk with my sister." She waved them away.

Once they were alone, Annani took both of Areana's hands. "Listen to me. You are an adult, and no one can force you into a union you do not consent to. You can tell Ahn that you have changed your mind."

She would rather die first. "I cannot. If I do not join Mortdh, he will go to war just to save his injured pride."

"War is inevitable. I know it, and our father knows it. Your sacrifice is only going to buy us time, but it is not going to avert it. Mortdh only pretended to accept Father's proposal."

After that rude 'used goods' comment, Areana had not listened to anything else that had been said, but she had seen Ahn and Mortdh shaking hands and had heard Ahn saying 'deal' before Mortdh and Navuh had departed.

Rearranging the folds of her skirt, she avoided Annani's eyes. "Time is valuable too. And what if the deal holds? Is it not worth it to at least give it a try?" She could be the hero, the one whose selfless sacrifice saved countless lives.

Maybe that was her purpose?

Annani grimaced. "There is a very slim chance that it will. Eventually, Mortdh will want more. He is insane—volatile and unpredictable."

Areana's gut twisted in fear. What if he was going to torture her? Or humiliate her publicly?

She had counted on Mortdh being uninterested in her and leaving her alone, and in that regard it seemed she had been right. Mortdh had barely spared her a glance. But what if he used her to get back at her father?

"Do you know if he is cruel to his women?" she asked in a whisper.

Everyone knew that Mortdh kept a large harem of human and immortal concubines. He was supposedly obsessed with proving his fertility by producing as many children as he could.

Before the ban on taking human partners had been lifted, Mortdh had not fathered even one child, and it was not for lack of trying with various lesser goddesses.

"I did not hear any rumors of cruelty. I think he is mostly indifferent. He treats them like breeding stock." Annani winced. "I am so sorry. I should have not said that."

"No, that is okay. I can live with that. I do not need his love or his attention. On the contrary. The more he leaves me alone, the better. But I am afraid he is going to take his frustrations out on me." Areana looked down at their joined hands. "What if he wants to hurt me and humiliate me to get back at Father?"

"It is a possibility. That is why I think you need to give it some more thought."

It was too late for that.

"I am afraid that I am out of time. The caravan will probably leave tomorrow at sunrise, and I still need to pack a few things."

Annani narrowed her eyes and started tapping her foot on the floor. "You can ask to stay for the wedding. They can leave a small contingent of warriors to escort you, or Ahn can offer you his own guards. It is not an unreasonable request."

Any delay was a good one. Areana was in no hurry to

march to her doom. "I will ask Navuh. He seems like a reasonable man."

"And he obviously likes you." Annani smirked. "Did you hear him gasp when you looked at him?"

"I am afraid I did not. I was too distraught."

Annani's foot resumed its tapping. "You might want to cultivate his infatuation with you. Navuh can be a powerful ally."

"He is definitely more attractive than his father." Areana sighed. "Even though Navuh is only an immortal and Mortdh is a god, I think the son is more handsome, and he seems perfectly sane."

"I agree. But you need to be careful. Navuh seems to be loyal to his father, and if he is, you should not divulge anything that might get you in trouble with Mortdh. On the other hand, Navuh could be plotting behind Mortdh's back and working on shoring up his own power base. If that is indeed the case, he might be willing to help you."

Annani smiled and patted Areana's knee. "The thing about despots is that they do not inspire loyalty, only fear."

NAVUH

On the way back to their caravan, Mortdh had not said a word, his anger rolling off him in dark, poisonous fumes. Everyone, including the foot soldiers and the servants, knew to keep quiet when he got like that —a simmering volcano that could and would erupt at the slightest provocation.

As they neared the encampment, the smells of roasted game put a spring in the steps of the warriors and servants accompanying them. While the cooks had been busy preparing the evening meal, the wagon drivers and other servants had erected his grand tent in the center, with the many small ones surrounding it.

Because of the large number of men Navuh had brought with him, the caravan had to be parked outside the city limits. It would have been unsafe for a smaller one, but no band of bandits was stupid enough to attack an encampment full of trained warriors.

"That went well," Navuh said. "Ahn's offer was very generous. It is almost everything you wanted, Father."

"Not even close." Mortdh slammed his fist into the side

of the carriage, splintering the wood. "I agreed to his proposal to throw him off guard. We keep on building our army and getting ready to take over by force. I do not want to be king of the Northern Territory. I want what I have always wanted and what should have been my birthright. I want to rule over them all. Gods, immortals, and humans."

Navuh had not been expecting a different answer. "So what now?" he asked as they got out of the carriage.

Passing the encampment, they continued walking in the direction of Mortdh's flyer. "I left one of your less competent brothers in charge while I was gone. I need to get back. You will bring the caravan home."

That too had been expected.

What Navuh found surprising and most welcome, however, was that Mortdh was not taking the goddess with him in the flyer, even though he could have saved her the long and arduous land journey.

Still, he had to ask. "What about Areana?"

Mortdh waved a dismissive hand. "Bring her with you. I promised Ahn a joining ceremony in two moon cycles, but I have no intention of actually going through with it. Fuck Ahn. After the way he humiliated me, I plan on humiliating him by keeping his daughter as a concubine instead of an official mate."

That was good news. Without a mating ceremony, Mortdh would probably stick Areana in the harem and forget about her. As a precaution, though, Navuh pretended to be troubled by his father's declaration. "But she is a goddess. You always wanted a pureblooded child."

Mortdh clapped his back. "You are only an immortal, but I could not have asked for a more capable and enterprising son. You are my successor."

"Thank you, Father." Navuh bowed deeply and kissed

the back of Mortdh's hand. The lunatic loved those simpering displays of gratitude.

He watched Mortdh climb into the flyer. "I will collect the princess from her home tomorrow morning, and we will be on our way by midday."

Mortdh put his goggles on and leaned out. "There is no hurry. You can take the long way home. And if you happen to encounter bandits, let them have her." He smiled, but Navuh knew his father had not meant it as a joke.

"Yes, Father." He bowed again.

That was actually not a bad idea. He could hide Areana somewhere and tell Mortdh that she had been taken by bandits.

There were a couple of problems with that, though.

First, he had nearly a hundred people with him, many of them immortal warriors. It was not likely that bandits would attack such a large caravan, and it was even less likely they would succeed in taking Areana.

Staging it would be impossible.

Perhaps it could be done if he sent the caravan ahead and retained only a handful of warriors to escort Areana at a later date. The problem with that was that he would look like an incompetent fool for letting Ahn's daughter be taken.

His reputation would be tarnished beyond repair.

As one who had lofty aspirations of becoming a ruler, Navuh needed to cultivate his image, inspiring respect and fear, not ridicule.

But what if he went ahead with the caravan and left her behind with a minimal escort? That could work, but then he would be putting her in real danger.

There had to be another way.

As Mortdh took to the sky, Navuh waved and smiled like a dutiful son was expected to. But as soon as the flyer disappeared from sight, he wiped the smile off his face and walked into the night, instead of heading toward the encampment.

In order to think, he needed a quiet walk.

What if he returned home with the caravan, going as fast as possible, and then took the flyer back to pick up Areana?

He could tell Mortdh that he was worried about her traversing the distance with only a small contingent of warriors. And if Mortdh refused to lend him the flyer, claiming that he did not care what happened to her, Navuh could come up with a good reason why losing Areana was a bad idea.

It was simple really.

All he had to say was that it would reflect poorly on Mortdh, making him the target of ridicule.

Then when Navuh caught up with Areana, he could eliminate her escort, take her to some hiding place, and then return home, claiming that he had been too late. That way it would not be his fault that she had been taken, but Mortdh's.

Doable, but still problematic.

A goddess was not easy to hide. Areana's glow was not as strong as some of the other gods and goddesses, but it was still there, and she was too weak of a goddess to be able to control it. He would have to keep her in isolation, which was a problem, since he could not see to her needs while attending to his father, and he could not entrust servants with such a secret.

The biggest issue, however, was convincing her to cooperate.

If Areana was anything like her half-sister, she would have jumped on the opportunity and welcomed the adventure. But Areana was gentle and timid and scared of her own shadow.

Besides, too many things could go wrong with this plan, and if Mortdh got a whiff of it, he would not hesitate to execute his own son for treason.

Unfortunately, it was back to the previous plan—getting rid of his father, and sooner rather than later.

AREANA

"Here, it is ready." Annani handed Areana a small scroll. "See if you approve."

If Areana had ever wondered why her father adored Annani and was so proud of her, she had gotten her answer that evening. The girl was a born strategist, and her understanding of politics was astounding. Areana had a feeling that young Annani had a better grasp of it than their father.

But then again, Annani was a risk taker while Ahn had to be more careful. She was not as rash as she appeared, though. Every step was carefully calculated. Annani was just faster than most at examining all the angles and evaluating all the possible pitfalls.

The first thing she had done was to verify that Mortdh had left in his flying boat. Then she made sure that Navuh had been left behind to lead the caravan back home.

Next, they had a brainstorming session about the best way to approach Navuh about allowing Areana to stay for the wedding.

And lastly, Annani even wrote the note a courier was

going to deliver to Navuh, asking him for a meeting. Or rather several notes, since she had written and then discarded at least five.

Annani collected the pieces of parchment strewn over her bed. "I think it sounds respectful but not simpering, and it hints at your interest in him."

"I am not interested in Navuh, or anyone else."

The princess shook her head. "It is a game, Areana. And the sooner you learn to play it, the better. You need to pretend to like him." Annani's lips curled in a smirk. "But I have a feeling it is not going to be difficult for you to pull off."

Areana sighed. "I will do my best."

Annani would never understand. Only those who had experienced the loss of a truelove mate or a child could do so.

The constant pain made pretending and playing games exceedingly difficult.

More than seven decades had passed since Ahnon had crossed to the other side—the mythical place beyond the veil where she hoped one day to join him—but the intensity of her grief had not diminished by much. Areana still woke up every morning and cried her eyes out because he was not there next to her.

Sleep was her only respite. In dreamland, Ahnon was alive, and they were still together. Unfortunately, her body refused to stay asleep for more than six hours.

Unfurling the scroll, Areana read Annani's note.

Dear Lord Navuh,

I would very much like to have an audience with you before our departure. Could you please come to see me at my house later tonight? It is imperative that I speak to you in private. I would have gladly come to you, but since your

*caravan is camped outside the city walls, it is not safe for me
to do so.*

Please give the courier your answer.

Respectfully,
  Areana

"It seems fine." She rerolled the scroll. "Do you think he
will come? What if he does not want to see me?"

"Pfft." Annani waved a dismissive hand. "Trust me, he
will come running, out of curiosity if not for any other
reason. Except, we both know why he is going to eagerly
accept your invitation." She waggled her brows.

Areana lowered her eyes. "I hope he will not expect
amorous favors."

"And what if he does? You do not have to do anything
you do not want to. Just show him some interest, compli-
ment him on this or that, and hint that you might be interested in some future time. That should do it. He is going to
be like wet clay in your hands."

Annani put too much confidence in Areana's manipulative skills.

"I do not know. Navuh is smart, and I am sure many
females try to gain his favor. He must be used to that.
Besides, I am not a temptress. I never was. I would not
know the first thing about it."

Taking her hand, Annani gave it a little squeeze. "You
are a goddess, Areana. You are beautiful and kind, and
Navuh seems infatuated with you. Have a little faith in
your feminine power. I know you are out of practice, and
that you are still grieving. But you are not dead. You are
still a woman with a woman's needs, or rather a goddess
with a goddess's needs. Some things should come naturally
to you."

Areana shook her head. "I will not get intimate with Navuh, if that is what you are suggesting. Not in exchange for two more moon cycles of freedom, or two years, or two decades. That part of me died seventy-one years ago, and unlike my body, my soul does not possess miraculous healing abilities."

5

NAVUH

avuh prided himself on his ability to anticipate other people's moves, but getting an invitation from Areana had taken him completely by surprise.

What did she want?

It sure as hell was not about her suddenly realizing that she found him irresistible. If it were any other female, he could have believed that, but not Areana, who had not spared any male a glance since her mate had been killed.

Such loyalty was admirable, if misplaced.

The god had allowed himself to get captured and decapitated by humans. Ahnon had been a weakling.

Sweet, soft Areana was so defenseless. A female like her needed a strong male by her side. Someone who would protect her and keep her safe. Thankfully, she had stayed home the day her mate had been murdered. Navuh shuddered as he imagined what would have been done to her by those bandits if she had joined him.

"Tell your lady I will arrive within an hour." He dismissed the courier.

The man bowed. "Thank you, my lord. Would you require directions to my lady's house?"

"That will not be necessary. I know the way."

Areana did not reside in a temple, but her home was open to every widow and orphan who needed help. Her funding must come from the palace because her worshipers were not the kind who brought gifts.

The courier bowed again. "I will deliver your message with due haste, my lord."

Given that Areana's house was about twenty minutes away on horseback, Navuh did not have much time to get ready. He washed in cold water because there was no time for the servants to heat it up for him, he shaved even though he had shaved that morning, and he put on a fresh tunic—black, of course, like all of his clothing, but with gold embroidery on the sleeves.

He liked to dress well, and his clothes were made by the best seamstresses money could buy. There was an element of vanity to it, as looking good pleased him, but that was not the main reason. As a non-god holding a god's position, Navuh needed every advantage available to him.

Then again, he did not want to appear soft or overly indulgent, especially not to Areana, which meant that he was not going to take the carriage.

Accompanied only by two warriors, he arrived at her place on horseback. Naturally, he left the guards in the goddess's front yard and entered her home alone.

The maid who opened the door bowed deep. "Good evening, Lord Navuh. My lady awaits your arrival in her reception room."

He followed the human inside, wondering if she was one of the widows Areana had taken under her wing. The woman was not old by human standards, but she was not young either.

What would become of them once their lady was gone?

It was none of his concern. If Areana did not arrange for someone else to take over, Ahn would have to do it for her.

As he entered her reception room, Areana rose to her feet with a forced smile on her beautiful face.

He could sense tension rolling off her in jagged waves.

"Thank you for coming to see me," she said in such a small voice that it was barely above a whisper.

He bowed with more respect than he had given her father. "It is my pleasure, Lady Areana. Receiving a summons from one of the most beautiful goddesses was a most pleasant surprise."

Her eyes widened. "It was not a summons. It was an invitation." She turned to her maid. "Please, bring in the refreshments, Manin."

"Yes, my lady." The woman scurried away.

"Would you care to join me at the table?" Areana waved in the direction of an intimate seating arrangement. Two low overstuffed chairs flanked a small round table that was covered with a blue tablecloth. A silver candleholder and two silver place settings made it look festive.

"I would love to."

"I asked my cook to prepare a light meal for us."

She wanted something from him, but, unfortunately, her scent did not indicate that her wish was carnal in nature.

Usually, women responded to him with a mix of fear and desire. It was a potent aphrodisiac to an immortal male's predatory nature. But Areana's scent lacked both. She was anxious, but not afraid, and definitely not aroused.

It was disappointing, but not unexpected.

A goddess who had remained chaste for more than seven decades must have deadened that part of herself. It was a shame to waste such beauty. The question was whether he could do something about it—light up the spark that had been extinguished by grief.

Perhaps an opportunity would present itself on the way. Areana required gentle coaxing, and that meant he would have to take his time with her, which was all right.

Unlike his father, Navuh was a very patient male.

"It is very kind of you." He waited until Areana was seated before taking the other chair.

"Would you care for some wine?" She lifted a silver decanter.

"Please." He offered her his goblet. "What can I do for you, Lady Areana?"

Her hand trembled only a little as she poured the wine. Navuh was glad to note that she was much less nervous around him than she had been around Mortdh.

"Just Areana, if it is agreeable to you."

Navuh smiled. "It is. And you can drop the lord too." He liked it when she called him lord, but he had no choice but to respond in kind.

She took a sip of the wine, put the goblet down, lifted it again, and took another sip, then put it down and did not look up. "I would very much like to attend my sister's joining ceremony. Would it be possible for you to leave without me? I am sure my father can provide me with an escort."

Navuh could barely stifle a wolfish grin. This was perfect. By the time Areana arrived at court, Mortdh would have forgotten all about her. In the meantime, Navuh might figure out how to hasten his plans to get rid of his father. "What date is the ceremony scheduled for?"

"Six weeks from today."

He frowned, pretending to think it over. The six weeks' wait for the upcoming joining ceremony, and then the long journey up north, would give him more time to come up with a plan. "My father would not appreciate it." His father could not care less. "But I think I can persuade him that it will be good for his public image to allow you to attend the joining ceremony. However, if I am to agree, I need to know for sure that your father is going to provide you with a proper escort. If anything were to happen to you, it would be my head on the line." Not really. If Areana fell into the hands of bandits, Mortdh would probably congratulate him on a job well done.

The one who wanted her to arrive safely and unharmed was Navuh, but he could not tell her that. Not yet.

Hopefully, by the time Areana arrived at court, he would have already taken over his father's domain. She would not have to face Mortdh at all.

For the first time since he had seen her at court, Areana smiled, taking his breath away. It was like an inner light had awakened inside her. Even her skin's glow became brighter.

"Thank you." She leaned toward him. "You have no idea what this means to me. I already spoke with Ahn, and he promised me a retinue of warriors. It will also give me time to pack. I was running around like a mad woman, trying to decide what to take and what to leave behind. Not to mention putting my house in order so my widows and orphans are taken care of." Areana was talking so fast that she ran out of breath.

Smiling, he put his hand over hers. "Breathe, Areana."

Instead of doing as he had instructed, she stopped breathing altogether.

During the mere seconds it took her to regain her composure and suck in a breath, Navuh could have sworn that Areana's scent of arousal momentarily flickered to life and then blinked out again just as soon as it ignited.

Another god or immortal, one who was not as attuned to her as he was, would have missed it.

With a soft blush coloring her pale cheeks pink, Areana withdrew her hand and wrapped it around her goblet. "I owe you a debt of gratitude, Lord Navuh."

This time he did not even try to stifle the predatory smirk curling up the corners of his mouth. "It is my pleasure to grant you your wishes, Lady Areana."

And my own.

When Navuh became ruler of the Northern Territory, no one would object to him mating Areana. Not even Ahn. The leader would be grateful to him for getting rid of Mortdh and restoring peace. And now that Ahn had given Mortdh sovereignty over the region, he could not take it back once Mortdh was gone.

As Mortdh's official successor, Navuh would inherit the deal.

6

AREANA

A pang of sorrow pierced Areana's heart as she followed the guard into the royal gardens. For years, she had dreamed about strolling through them arm in arm with her father. In the fantasy, he was smiling at her with appreciation in his eyes. That was the most she had ever hoped for.

Fatherly love was too much of a leap even for a dream.

"There you are!" Annani rushed toward her. Pulling her into a quick embrace, she whispered in her ear, "I am dying of curiosity."

Areana affected a puzzled expression. "About what?"

With a quick wave of her hand, Annani dismissed the guard. "You may return to your station."

"Good day, my lady." He bowed and turned on his heel.

Tugging on Areana's hand, Annani led her to a shaded gazebo. "I want to hear every little detail."

The table was set with refreshments, and two colorful pillows had been placed on the stone bench—one yellow and the other blue—which meant that no one else was going to join them.

A few paces away, two guards were standing watch.

Areana chose the blue one to sit on. "Thank you for inviting me. I have never been to the royal gardens before."

"That is a shame. Unfortunately, due to security concerns, we cannot hold festivities in the garden." Annani lifted a carafe and poured a red liquid into two goblets. "It is not wine, in case you were wondering. It is pomegranate juice."

As if she could not smell the difference. Areana was a weak goddess, but she was not entirely devoid of enhanced senses. "Thank you. Pomegranate juice is a perfect complement for a late morning meal."

Annani lifted her goblet, took a few sips and then put it down. "I think so too. Now tell me, how did it go with Navuh? Did he agree?"

"Yes."

Annani clapped her hands. "This is absolutely fabulous!" She leaned and wrapped her arms around Areana. "I am so happy that you are going to be at my joining ceremony." Letting go, she winked. "And that you have an additional one and a half moon cycles of freedom."

"More." Areana smiled. "Navuh agreed to let palace guards accompany me to Mortdh's stronghold instead of leaving behind some of his warriors. If I do not hurry, which I have no intention of doing, the journey will take a very long time."

For some reason, Annani did not seem happy about that. "I do not like it. I will tell Father to double your escort and provide you with his best warriors."

"Why?"

"It might be nothing. But I find it suspicious that Navuh was so accommodating."

The princess's meaning was quite clear. "Do you think Mortdh wants to get rid of me even before I get there?"

"It is a remote possibility, but I would rather err on the side of caution."

"I do not think Navuh means me harm."

Annani sighed. "He might not, but he is Mortdh's lackey."

That was a misconception. Navuh was no one's lackey, and whoever thought that either did not know him, or chose to ignore what was clearly evident to anyone who paid attention.

Areana might be a weak goddess with mediocre senses, but she was a good judge of character.

Gods relied too heavily on their sense of smell and ignored clues that smart humans picked up with ease. Areana had dismal godly powers, but she had developed excellent observational skills.

Still, although Annani was wrong about Navuh, Areana did not wish to contradict her. This opportunity to form a relationship with her half-sister was the only good thing to come out of the big mess that Ahn had cooked up. Areana was not going to risk antagonizing her most powerful ally.

Well, Navuh might turn out to be one as well, but she could not be sure of his motives or his reliability. He was opportunistic, and his actions or lack thereof served his own interest.

Navuh was not going to help her out of the goodness of his heart.

Annani, on the other hand, was exactly who she seemed to be. There was no subterfuge behind her actions, and she was not looking to gain an advantage by befriending Areana.

"Navuh seems to like me." She had not wanted to talk about this, but a change of topic was needed. "I am not sure he is attracted to me, though. I did not smell any scent of arousal."

That was only partially true.

The strong scents of confidence and determination he was broadcasting could have overpowered every other scent that he might have been emitting, but those two were enough to awaken her dormant feminine needs.

Navuh's scent was the most powerfully male one that Areana had ever encountered.

Naturally, she had quashed that tiny flame as soon as it had been ignited. It had been most inappropriate, and not only because she still grieved for Ahnon.

Annani waved a hand. "Some people know how to control their scents. With Mortdh as his father, I bet Navuh had no choice but to develop the ability to mask his scent. If I were him, I would definitely do everything I could to camouflage my feelings. Otherwise, I doubt Navuh would have risen to such a position of power in Mortdh's court."

It made sense. Navuh had to appear as the dutiful son, always doing his father's bidding, but Areana suspected that he had his own agenda in the grand scheme of things. That cunning intelligence still shone in his eyes just as brightly as she had remembered.

"It is possible. But it is also irrelevant. I am to mate his father. The important thing is that Navuh agreed to let me stay. He also promised to convince Mortdh that it was a good idea to let me attend your joining ceremony. For that, I am beyond grateful."

Areana took a deep breath. "It will give me time to put my house in order. I did not have enough time to find and train a capable administrator to take over for me and see to the needs of my orphans and widows. Now I can resume the search."

"Do you have anyone in mind?"

By Annani's slight grimace, it was evident she did not

want the job. Not that Areana would have ever suggested it. Annani had to learn how to take care of all people in her territory. Smaller causes were better handled by other gods.

The problem was that Areana could not think of anyone who would want to take over hers. They would tell her that the widows should seek help at the temples, which was what most of those in need of assistance did.

"I asked my mother, but she declined, and none of the other goddesses will want the job. My other option is to hire an immortal to manage my place. I have interviewed several, but none were a good fit. Now I have enough time to resume the search and train my replacement."

Annani nodded. "It is a good idea, but you need someone to supervise her. The palace is providing funds for the charity, and those could be easily misappropriated by a hired hand."

She had not thought of that. "That is true. But who can do that?"

"I can ask Khiann. As a merchant, I am sure he knows all about keeping employees honest."

7

ESAG

"*H*ello, my handsome intended," Ashegan greeted Esag with a smile.

What was going on? He was so used to a sour-faced welcome that this was entirely unexpected. No complaints, though. He was about to make some wise comment about it, when she proceeded to wrap her arms around him and kissed him right on the lips.

Esag sucked in a breath, in part because her soft breasts were pressed against his chest, and in part because she had never been so nice to him before.

Whatever the reason, he was not going to waste the opportunity to cop a feel. Grabbing her ample ass in both hands, he pressed her tighter against him and swiveled his hips, half expecting her to push him away.

For an immortal, Ashegan was not very sexual. Even though they had been engaged since they were little kids, he had not gotten more than a few kisses from her, and none were overly passionate.

Surprisingly, instead of pushing him away, she pressed herself closer to him and kissed him with even more fervor. In no time, his fangs punched down, and he accidentally nicked her.

Cringing, Esag leaned back, expecting a tirade about how he should be more careful.

"Oh, Esag," she husked. "I wish we were already joined. I cannot wait to be with you."

So that was what Ashegan was after.

As long as she kept kissing him and rubbing her breasts against him, he was going to agree to anything she wanted.

"Maybe if I get a little taste, I will be more motivated to hasten the joining."

With a coy smile, Ashegan took his hand and led him to her bed. "And perhaps if I get a taste of you, I will crave more."

Thank you, dear Fates.

The next morning, Esag strode into Khiann's office an hour late. "It is all your fault."

Khiann cocked a brow. "How is it my fault that you are late?"

"Ashegan wants to have our joining ceremony a week after yours and Annani's." He plopped into a chair. "She's caught the joining bug. The best I can do is convince her that she needs more time to plan the party."

Khiann, who had been grinning like a fool ever since Mortdh's departure, made an admirable effort to frown, but the result was not very convincing. "You knew it was coming sooner or later."

"I was hoping for later." Esag groaned. "I need a drink."

That was what he had been saying for years, so he kept at it even though it was no longer true. After the taste Ashegan had given him last night, Esag was all for hastening the joining.

For a change, she had been most generous with her affections.

"I agree." Khiann pushed to his feet. "This calls for a visit to a tavern."

Esag lifted a brow. "Is it okay with Annani? I was under the impression that she wants you to spend every free moment with her. She will not be happy about you going to a tavern."

He was not one to criticize, but the truth was that Khiann was slacking. He was not training, and he was barely putting in any work in the office for his father.

"She is meeting Areana this morning, so I am excused. I thought to go over the ledgers, but I am not in the mood for it. A beer in Ninkasi's tavern sounds much better."

Esag grinned. "Mind if I invite a couple of friends?"

"Are we celebrating?" Khiann paused at the door.

"Yes, we are. This is a perfect opportunity to toast your upcoming joining ceremony and my impending funeral."

"You just like to complain." Khiann put his goggles on before pushing the door open. "I think that secretly you cannot wait to join Ashegan."

"Right." He followed Khiann out and squinted.

As a third generation immortal, the harsh sunlight did not bother Esag as much as it bothered a god or a first generation immortal. There were some advantages to having diluted blood.

The disadvantages, however, outweighed the advantages and then some. Esag's thralling and shrouding abilities were mediocre at best, and he was not nearly as fast as a first generation immortal. But that was not as important as the social status. The more diluted the blood, the lower the social standing.

It was not official, and supposedly no one kept records, but every immortal knew precisely where he or she stood in comparison to others. Even the humans treated first generation immortals with more respect than the subsequent ones.

It was not hard to guess.

The further down the line an immortal was, the less his or her features reflected godly heritage.

With his red hair, Esag was lucky in that regard. Very few immortals inherited the unique color from the gods, but even fewer inherited the pale hair and skin. No immortal, though, not even first generation, inherited the luminescent skin. That was why an immortal could not pass for a god. A god, however, could pass for an immortal by consciously dimming the glow.

"Where are you going?" Khiann's mother asked as they headed for the front door.

"To celebrate my upcoming joining ceremony, as well as Esag's."

Yaeni smiled. "Congratulations, Esag. When is the happy occasion, and are we invited?"

As if his or Ashegan's parents were going to miss an opportunity to show off their god friends to their immortal and human ones. Not that Khiann's parents were more than casually acquainted with Esag's or Ashegan's.

"Of course you are. I do not have an exact date yet, but Ashegan is in a hurry. I think a month after Khiann and Annani's joining."

Yaeni lifted a brow. "Is there a reason for the rush?"

"I wish." Esag snorted.

He would not have minded having a child, but Ashegan was in no hurry for that, only for the joining.

"Having children is a blessing, but it is also a lot of responsibility." Yaeni clapped Khiann on his back. "And just when you think they are all grown up and are going to repay you by easing your workload and helping you run the business, they fall in love and neglect their duties."

The barb was delivered with a smile and in a loving tone, but it was a barb nonetheless.

Khiann grimaced. "I know I have been slacking lately, Mother. I promise to try and do better."

She waved a dismissive hand. "While your head is still in the clouds, you are probably wasting your time in the office anyway. Have fun with your intended. Your poor father is going to pick up the slack." She sighed dramatically.

"You are in a needling mood today."

Stretching up on her toes to reach his face, Yaeni kissed Khiann's cheek. "Just so you are mentally prepared. Two weeks after the joining ceremony we expect you to get back to work."

"I will. I promise."

8

ANNANI

*T*wo things cast dark shadows over Annani's happy bubble, preventing her from soaring on a cloud of bliss.

One was the worry for Areana and her future with Mortdh, and the other was Gulan's gloomy mood that seemed to be getting worse by the day instead of getting better. The girl went about her duties with a hunched back and eyes that were misted with tears.

"What has eyes but does not have a face?" Annani asked, hoping to get a smile out of her friend.

"I do not know, my lady."

"Oh, come on, Gulan. This is an old one."

"I do not know it, my lady."

"A rotten apple!" Annani laughed at her own joke.

Gulan did not even crack a smile.

"All right, how about this. I lose a head in the morning and get it back at night. What am I?"

Gulan shrugged. "I do not know."

Lifting a pillow from her bed, Annani tossed it to Gulan. "Here is a clue."

"A pillow?"

"Yes, you got it."

Gulan still did not smile. "Can I take a day off, my lady? I wish to go home and spend a day with my family. Now that you have the Odus, you do not need me as much."

"Of course you can go home if you so wish. But I always need you, Gulan. The Odus are no substitute for my best friend."

That wrested a ghost of a smile from the girl. "Thank you, my lady. But you have master Khiann now. I am sure he is much better company than plain old me."

Annani walked over to Gulan and pulled her into her arms. "I love Khiann with all my heart, but some things a girl can only talk about with her best friend. No one can ever replace you."

"That is very kind of you to say, my lady." Gulan sniffled.

Annani frowned. This was not about feeling unneeded. "What is going on? You are more mopey than ever."

"I am sorry, my lady. I cannot help it." Gulan sniffled louder.

Annani pushed her friend toward the bed. "Come, sit with me and tell me what is wrong."

Impersonating a sack of potatoes, Gulan let herself get pushed and seated.

"Is it about Esag?" Annani asked.

Gulan nodded. "He and Ashegan are going to have their joining ceremony a month after yours and Khiann's."

It was not news to Annani. Esag had told Khiann, who had told her. But she was sure no one had had a chance to inform Gulan. News did not spread that quickly. "Where did you hear that?"

Pulling a washrag from her pocket, Gulan wiped her tears and then blew her nose. "Ashegan is telling everyone about it. Naila heard it from her sister, who had heard it from one of Ashegan's friends, and she told me."

"I see." Annani wracked her brain for something comforting to say. "It must be hard for you. But on the other hand, maybe it is better this way."

Lifting her face, Gulan looked at her with a pair of tear-filled eyes. "How can it be better?"

"I think that as long as he is not mated, you harbor an irrational hope that he will choose you over her. And every day that passes with him not showing any such intent is causing you more pain. Once that door is permanently closed, you can finally move on."

"Move on where?"

"With your life. You can start looking at other guys. I can tell you which of the palace guards are neither mated nor promised to anyone, and you can have your pick of the finest of males. I did not see even one guard who is unappealing, and they are all tall because they are chosen for their intimidating statures."

She should have thought about that sooner and made some inquiries. A little prompting, or just a hint that Gulan was available and looking, would have been enough. She was well liked and respected among the palace staff.

Her friend sniffled again. "None have ever paid me any attention. I am big and graceless and unfeminine. Besides, even though Esag does not have real feelings for me, I have feelings for him. It is not something that I can just exorcize with a wave of my hand."

Hmm, that was not a bad idea.

Maybe Annani could arrange an exorcizing session. She could pay one of those fake fortunetellers to come to the palace and give Gulan an encouraging foretelling about a handsome immortal that she was going to meet and fall in love with in the future.

Hope was a powerful thing, and right now her friend needed an infusion of it.

"You know, Gulan. I believe every immortal has her or his destined mate. They can be separated by land or by time and not know of each other's existence. Some might give up and settle for what is near and immediate, while others will keep on looking. I think that you have settled for Esag because he was here and because he paid you attention. Your truelove mate is somewhere out there, or perhaps he is yet to be born. As an immortal, you are not bound by time like a human. All you need is faith and patience and you will find him."

Gulan dabbed at her eyes with the rag. "Most gods, as well as immortals, do not find their trueloves."

"That is because they lack both faith and patience."

Shaking her head, Gulan sighed. "I can be patient, but I am afraid I do not have faith."

Aha, that was where Annani had been leading with her romantic speech. "What if you could see into the future?"

"Do you mean like consulting a soothsayer?"

"Why not?"

Gulan snorted. "They are all fakes, my lady. They tell you what you want to hear. That is how they make a living."

"You are right about most. But I heard of an old human who has foretold many things that have come to pass. I will invite her to the palace to give us both a reading."

Gulan shook her head. "If you wish to throw away your money, it is your choice, my lady. But it would be better spent on charity."

"But it is charity, my dear friend. The old human is blind, and this is how she puts food on her table." Annani clasped Gulan's hands. "We do not need to take the fore-telling seriously. We are going to have some fun while being charitable at the same time. If you wish, we can also invite Areana to join us. She could use a few laughs herself."

"Can I bring Tula?"

"Of course. The more the merrier."

9

GULAN

"*I* am so excited," Tula rubbed her hands. "Will the fortuneteller tell my fortune too?"

Gulan shook her head. "It is all nonsense. No one knows the future."

Her little sister lifted her chin and huffed. "You are no fun."

"Maybe, but at least I am not going to be disappointed when nothing the old crone has to say comes true. She is a human and can spout all the fancy stories she wants because she knows she will not live long enough to be held accountable for her lies."

Tula shrugged. "Whatever. I am just happy that you got me invited too. After I tell everyone I went to a party with the princess and her sister, I will become the most popular girl in school."

Gulan laughed. "Silly girl. No one is going to believe you. Besides, Annani might ask us to keep it a secret."

"Is that why we are going to Lady Areana's house and not the palace? Because the princess does not want anyone to know she had her fortune read by a human?"

"No, that is not the reason. Lady Areana insisted on hosting our little party."

That was what Annani had told her, but maybe Tula was right, and the princess did not want anyone to know.

Smart.

People would make fun of her for believing in such silliness. Only humans consulted soothsayers. Gods and immortals had the perspective of time to know better.

As they arrived at Lady Areana's house, Tula ran up to the royal carriage that was parked in front of it. "It is so beautiful." She ran her hands over the carvings on its side.

Watching her, the palace guards posted outside the house smiled indulgently.

"Come on." Gulan tugged on her sister's tunic.

"Are we late?"

"Just a little. I blame your short legs." At twelve, Tula's height was slightly below that of an average-sized girl. Compared to Gulan, though, she was tiny and had a hard time keeping up.

"Hello, Gulan." Gumer opened the door for her and then ruffled Tula's hair. "Sprout."

With an indignant huff, Tula flicked his hand off. "I am not a sprout. I am a young lady."

Gulan rolled her eyes. What was it with short girls and big attitudes? Tula was no princess, and yet she acted like one.

A maid led them to where Areana and Annani were seated on plush cushions. Between them, a low round table held several plates filled with nuts and cut fruit. There were also five goblets and two pitchers, one filled with juice and the other with diluted wine.

Pushing on Tula's shoulder to remind her of her manners, Gulan curtsied. "Thank you for inviting us into your home, Lady Areana. This is my sister Tula."

"It is my pleasure." The goddess patted the pillow next to her. "Come, sit with me, Tula."

Gulan sucked in a breath. She was used to Annani treating her as an equal, but none of the other gods and goddesses ever did.

She put a hand on Tula's shoulder. "Thank you, but my sister and I do not deserve the honor. We will stay back there." She pointed to where Areana's maid was standing.

The goddess waved a dismissive hand. "You are my guests. Come, Tula. You will sit right here, and your sister can sit next to Annani."

Tula did not need a third invitation. Wiggling from under Gulan's hand, she rushed to sit down on the cushion Areana had indicated. "Thank you. I am so excited. When is the soothsayer coming?"

Areana patted her shoulder. "I sent my carriage for her. She should be arriving soon."

"Is she very old?"

"For a human, she is. And she is also blind."

Tula shook her head. "How sad."

"It is just the way it is," Gulan said.

As they heard the front door open, all eyes turned to watch the old woman lumber inside. Leaning on the carriage driver, she looked at them with a pair of milky eyes that were obviously blind but oddly penetrating.

"Welcome to my home." Areana rose to her feet and took the fortuneteller's elbow. "Let me help you to your seat." She led the woman to the only chair, then helped her sit down. "Would you like something to drink?"

"Thank you, my lady. You are most kind."

"Pomegranate juice or diluted wine?" Areana's maid rushed to serve.

"The juice. I am afraid my old body does not tolerate wine well."

After everyone's goblets had been filled, the soothsayer took a few sips, and then turned to their hostess as if she could see her. "Lady Areana, am I right?"

"Yes, you are."

"May I start with your fortune?"

Areana exchanged knowing looks with Annani. "Yes, you may."

"You have a long journey ahead of you."

Gulan smirked. That was not a prediction. Everyone knew that Areana was going to Mortdh's stronghold in the north and that it was far away.

"A heavy burden rests on your shoulders. You have a most important task. Your gentle soul and soft heart will guide you on your path. I see a child in your future. A son will be born to you and the rogue. Stay strong and true and teach him right from wrong."

Talk about vague and uninspired. Areana was to mate Mortdh, the rogue, and she might have a son with him, whom she would have to teach right from wrong like every mother should. Gulan could have made the same prediction with as much chance of it becoming true.

"What about me?" Tula asked.

The soothsayer looked in Tula's direction and shook her head. "I am afraid the spirits have nothing to say about you, child. Perhaps you are too young, and your future has not been written yet."

"Do the spirits have something to say about me?" Gulan asked, injecting her tone with as much sarcasm as she dared in front of the two goddesses.

For a few long moments, the soothsayer pretended to listen to voices only she could hear. "Yes, they do."

Despite her skepticism, Gulan could not help the little flutter in her heart. "What is it?"

"Many years from now, in a land across the ocean, you will find truelove with a gentle giant of a man."

Gulan lifted a brow, and then remembered that the woman was blind and dropped it. "That is all? Do I have an important task to fulfill too?"

"The spirits did not tell me. You will have to find out for yourself."

"But they told you that I would find my truelove mate and that he was going to be tall?"

The fortuneteller lifted her slim arm over her head. "A giant of a man," she corrected.

Right. Annani must have told the woman that Gulan was big. In fact, the goddess had probably told the sooth-sayer what Gulan wanted to hear.

Annani clapped her hands. "Fabulous foretelling. Now it is my turn."

The old woman turned her sightless eyes to the goddess and then shook her head. "My deepest apologies, my lady, but I am afraid two fortunes are all I can do today. Talking to the spirits is not as easy as it seems. It takes a toll on me, and this old body is not what it used to be."

Pushing up to her shaky legs, the old woman braced her hand on the chair's back and hunched her shoulders. "Could the kind man take me back to my home? I need to lie down. When I am better, I will come to the palace to foretell your glorious future."

If Annani was disappointed, she hid it well. "Of course. I would not want you to overtax yourself on my behalf." She winked at her companions and mouthed, "I do not want her premature death on my conscience."

NAVUH

"Good job, men," Navuh addressed the small crowd of warriors, drivers, and other servants assembled in the courtyard of his father's palace. "As promised, you each get a bonus for every day shaved off the journey. This must be a new record for a caravan crossing between the southern and northern capitals." He clapped his hands, and the crowd erupted in cheers.

Over the years, Navuh had learned how to motivate people to do what he wanted them to, and to do it well.

The best motivator was giving people a worthy goal and convincing them that what they were doing was important. The cause did not even need to be real or true. It was enough that it was believable and inspired strong feelings.

Another, which he used today, was a combination of praise and monetary compensation. Those were the easiest and most immediate since they did not require much thought or elaborate setup.

Fear was the strongest motivator, but it did not inspire loyalty. Still, it was a crucial component in every good ruler's arsenal of tools. As a deterrent to others, traitors and dissidents had to be dealt with quickly and ruthlessly.

Navuh had his father to thank for those lessons. Mortdh was smart and had thousands of years of experience managing people, or rather exploiting them, while convincing them that they should be grateful for his benevolent guidance.

Some of it he attributed to Mortdh's personal charisma, but most of it was the result of calculated steps and clever propaganda.

Navuh's hatred for his father did not blind him to the fact that there was a lot he could learn from him.

Regrettably, Mortdh did not volunteer information freely.

It had taken decades of observation and careful coaxing to get Mortdh to reveal his secrets, and it would take many more to learn them all—especially their people's history, of which Mortdh had told him only very little.

But Navuh no longer had the luxury of time. He had to come up with a plan to get rid of Mortdh and implement it before Areana's arrival at his father's court.

Besides, by now he had probably learned enough of Mortdh's tricks to take over the rule of the north.

"According to my calculations, we arrived seven days earlier than scheduled. Which means each of you gets seven times the bonus."

He waited as more cheers followed, and then lifted his hand. "Go home, wash and rest, and tomorrow report to the treasury for your pay."

As the crowd slowly dispersed, Navuh headed to his father's reception chamber. He would have rather gone straight to his quarters and done precisely what he told the caravan staff to do, but Mortdh had to be informed of his arrival in person.

"You are back early," Mortdh said as Navuh entered.

"I did not wish to waste time, Father. I just wanted to inform you that I am back, and then to retire to my rooms and take a bath."

Mortdh waved his hand, dismissing everyone else from the room. "What did you do with Ahn's daughter?" he asked as soon as the servants had left.

Evidently, their spy network had not reported the news about Areana staying behind. Or maybe it was a test.

Mortdh liked playing games.

Navuh smiled evilly. "She begged me to let her stay for her sister's joining ceremony. I agreed on the condition that her father would supply her escort. I thought it played perfectly into your plans for humiliating Ahn. Leaving her behind without taking care of her travel arrangements is the ultimate insult."

As a growl started deep in Mortdh's throat, Navuh took an instinctive step back.

Had he made a mistake?

Impossible.

He had learned to anticipate Mortdh's responses a long time ago, and he had not been wrong in decades.

Mortdh waved his hand, sealing the chamber in a silencing shroud. "I am going to kill that fucker before he officially joins Annani." He pointed a finger at Navuh. "I want you to plan an assassination."

Stifling a relieved breath, Navuh shook his head. "The only way Khiann can be assassinated without us getting blamed for it is if he ventures outside the city walls. When he does, we can stage a bandit attack."

He did not think his father was brazen enough to take responsibility for the assassination—not with an inadequate army that could not defend him against a joint attack launched by the other gods.

"Do not mention his name in my presence!" Mortdh barked. "Is he not a merchant?" he added in a calmer voice.

"He is."

"Then he must leave the city at one point or another. My spies will inform me when he makes travel plans. Caravans take a long time to prepare, so he cannot just get up and go. We will have enough advance notice. In the meantime, I want you to assemble a unit of trustworthy warriors and train them for the mission."

"Yes, Father." Navuh bowed.

"You are dismissed."

"Thank you, Father."

It was not surprising that Mortdh did not want to get his hands dirty by killing the god himself. Besides, this way, if the plot was discovered, he could put the blame on Navuh's shoulders, and Navuh would have no way to dispute it.

It would be his word against that of a powerful god.

Back in his chambers, Navuh ordered a bath to be prepared for him and then waited for his servant to be done.

"Thank you, Ruhag. Make sure I am not disturbed," he dismissed the servant.

"Certainly, my lord. I will have a meal prepared for you and leave it in the front chamber."

"Thank you."

Navuh's servants were all well trained warriors who doubled as his bodyguards. With dozens of ambitious half-brothers, he could not be too careful.

With a sigh, he sank into the water, wetting every part of himself including his long hair. To wash away all the grime he'd accumulated, he would need to empty the bath and refill it with fresh water at least twice, but he was going to do it himself.

Privacy was a luxury that Navuh had missed on the road almost as much as he had missed a bath. He needed to think, and for that, he needed to be free of distractions.

Throughout the many days of travel, he had tried to come up with a good plan for eliminating his father and ensuring Areana's safety, as well as that of the rest of the realm, but none were foolproof.

There were only a couple of ways of doing so without being accused of killing a god, and patricide. One was to arrange an assassination like the one Mortdh planned for Khiann, and the other was tampering with his father's flyer.

The problem with the first one was that Mortdh was an incredibly powerful god and as suspicious as they came. Which meant that he could not be taken down by immortals. Before any of the assailants managed to land a blow, his father would freeze them in place and thrall them to attack each other.

Which left killing him in his sleep.

Except, Mortdh would have to be heavily drugged not to sense them coming. Regrettably, Navuh knew of no odorless and tasteless drug, which meant that this was out too.

It seemed like tampering with the flyer was his best bet. But Navuh was not sure a crash would kill Mortdh. The thing had to explode before it even hit the ground to ensure Mortdh's body would be completely incinerated. Other than cutting out his heart or beheading him, this was the only way to ensure that the damage was beyond his body's self-repairing capabilities.

GULAN

*A*nnani and Khiann's joining ceremony had been beautiful. The love between them had shone so brightly that even the most cynical of guests had been moved, especially during the exchange of vows.

Several had even shed a few tears.

Gulan had shed a lot, but not for the same reason.

Tonight, after she had helped Annani out of her ceremonial attire, Gulan was leaving.

She might never see her best friend again.

The smile she had plastered on her face was so fake, it would have never fooled Annani if her mind was not as full of Khiann as it was. Or maybe her lady was just too happy to notice.

Gods, it was so difficult to keep from crying openly when Gulan felt as if she were dying inside. With a tremendous effort, she held on until the preparations for the mating night were finished and she bade Annani goodnight. But as soon as the door to the newly-mated couple's bedchamber closed behind her, the tears burst free, running down her cheeks and wresting pitiful sobs out of her.

Leaving was so hard. But staying would be harder.

Thank the gods, Gulan did not encounter anyone as she ran all the way to the servants' quarters. In the privacy of her own room, she leaned against the closed door and cried even harder.

She was being ungrateful.

The private chamber that Gulan did not have to share with another maid was just one more kindness out of the many that her lady had bestowed upon her throughout the years. While the rest of the palace staff slept two and three to a room, Gulan had the entire bedchamber to herself.

And how was she repaying it?

By running away and leaving a cowardly note behind.

The decision to leave had been the hardest Gulan had ever made in her life, but an unavoidable one. The pain of losing Esag, or rather the dream of him, was too much for her to bear. If she stayed, she would have to watch him join with another, and Gulan knew she would not survive that.

It was better to start a new life somewhere far away from Esag.

She would go on an adventure and travel to distant lands. Until the pain subsided, Gulan would fill her life with the exploration of the different human cultures Esag had told her about. If traders went there on a regular basis, so could she. People who produced goods and engaged in trade could not be completely uncivilized. The gods' teachings must have reached them.

Wiping away her tears with the sleeve of her beautiful new dress, Gulan took a deep breath and sighed. After weeks of planning, it was finally time.

Maybe in a year or two, once she had healed enough,

she would come back and tell Annani about all she had seen.

She needed to get moving, though. The caravan she was joining was heading out at sunrise, which was in a couple of hours.

Pushing away from the door, Gulan walked over to her bed, took off the dress Annani had commissioned for her for the ceremony, folded it carefully, and put it on top of the mattress.

Where she was going, Gulan would have no need for it. In fact, since she was going as a young man, not a woman, she would have no need for any feminine garb.

It was quite ironic that after a lifetime of resenting her height and strength, she was taking advantage of both. The caravan organizer was always looking for capable, strong men who could lift heavy cargo and defend the caravan if needed.

Even Esag's combat training would come in handy.

Standing in front of a mirror with a pair of shears in hand, Gulan took hold of her thick braid and hesitated for only a moment before hacking it off. What was left fanned out around her face, the jagged edges looking as haggard and sad as her soul.

With several quick snips, she evened it out to look like an acceptable hairstyle for a man. Dipping her fingers in a pouch filled with soot, she smeared it over her chin. Hopefully, it would pass as a shadow of a beard.

Her face was still too feminine to belong to a male, but with her size, no one would question her gender. They would assume she was a young man with a girly face.

It happened.

The next step was to bind her breasts and put on the peasant clothes she had bought. Under the tunic, she tied a pouch full of coins. Some of it was what she had managed to save up, but most of it came from selling the necklace Annani had given her. It was enough to keep her fed for a year.

With what she was going to get paid for working in the caravan, Gulan had nothing to worry about—except for Tula, her parents, and Annani.

Leaving behind the people she loved was the hardest part. But they would manage without her—provided Annani was not too angry with her for running away and would help her family.

Gulan trusted that her lady's kind heart would not turn vindictive.

The truth was that Annani no longer needed her. With Khiann to keep her company and the Odus serving her lady's every need, a maid was superfluous. But even if Annani decided to send riders after her, she would not know in which direction Gulan was heading.

No one would expect her to choose the remote Nile valley as her final destination.

ESAG

*E*sag cringed under Khiann's hard glare. The god sitting behind the desk was not his friend. He was his employer, and he was angry. He had not even asked Esag to sit down.

"I need you to go find Gulan," Khiann said. "It is your fault that she ran away. If you had done what I asked of you and stopped toying with her feelings, she would still be here."

As if he needed another dose of guilt to feel appropriately chastised. "Can I see her note?" he asked.

She was probably hiding somewhere nearby. Gulan was a careful girl who was not brave enough to embark on a journey on her own. It was more Annani's style to do something so impulsive. The roads were not safe for a woman alone, and Gulan was well aware of that.

Khiann shook his head. "The note was addressed to Annani. I do not think Gulan wanted you to read it."

"But she must have mentioned me for you to accuse me of making her run away."

Khiann pinned him with another hard stare. "It is your fault, Esag. Gulan was in love with you."

"I am not responsible for her feelings. Besides, you know that I am trapped, and that I cannot do anything about my upcoming joining." He scratched his head. "I wish I could."

"Well, this is your chance. On Princess Annani's orders, you are leaving on a retrieval mission. Your upcoming nuptials will have to wait for your return."

Was Khiann offering him a way out of joining with Ashegan?

Did he want one?

Not really.

"So, if I understand you correctly, I am not to return unless I have Gulan with me?"

Khiann's lips lifted in a smirk. "Exactly."

If Esag's orders were not to return unless he had Gulan, he could pretend not to find her even if he did. He could take her somewhere where they could live together as a couple. Ashegan's family could not fault him or his parents for him leaving and then not returning. Not when his mission was on behalf of the princess.

But where could he take her?

Mortdh's territory was a possibility. The god's rumored insanity and his animosity toward Ahn had no real bearing on a couple of lowly immortals. They could probably get servants' positions, either in his court or in the house of some rich immortal who had gained Mortdh's favor.

Except, that would mean abandoning his family, which Esag was not keen on. He loved his parents and his sisters. Hell, he had been willing to mate the annoying Ashegan so they would have a better life. In that regard, nothing had changed. Well, except for Ashegan sweetening the deal by finally showing him some real affection.

Gulan was a great girl, and Esag liked her a lot, but the bottom line was that he did not love her enough to forsake his family for her.

That did not mean that he would not go looking for her, though. He had made this mess, and it was his duty to fix it. He would never forgive himself if something happened to her.

Stupid girl.

Why did she have to do something so dramatic?

"I will find her, and I will bring her home. Hopefully, she will come willingly. But if she does not, I am going to drag her back anyway."

Khiann's smile turned into a frown. "You are still going to mate Ashegan."

Esag nodded. "I like Gulan a lot. But I am not willing to leave everyone I love behind to be with her. I want to be near my parents and my sisters. I want to have family dinners and celebrations with them. I want to meet the miserable donkeys who are going to mate my sisters. And I want to be there when they have babies. And for that, I am even willing to tolerate Ashegan."

"I understand." Khiann shook his head. "You really should not have led Gulan on. You never loved her."

Esag looked down at his feet. "I thought I could have the best of both worlds—join with Ashegan and keep Gulan as a concubine. But I should have known better. Gulan is too proud to accept a secondary position."

"It is not about pride, Esag. Gulan loved you, and she was not willing to share you with another woman. Would you have been willing to share her?"

"She was not that kind of girl."

"Exactly. But we are wasting valuable time here." Khiann pulled a heavy money pouch from his pocket and handed it to Esag. "That should suffice to cover your expenses."

Weighing the pouch in his hand, Esag whistled. "This is enough to cover my expenses for a year."

"I hope it is not going to take you that long to find Gulan. However, since the princess insists that you take two warriors with you, you will incur higher expenses. Their wages are paid by Annani, but you will have to cover the costs of replacement horses if needed and feed them on the road."

Esag had not expected that. It was very kind of the princess, especially since she was so mad at him that she refused to see him, delegating all the arrangements as well as the chastising to Khiann. "I appreciate the princess's generosity."

"I will tell her you said that. Maybe it will mollify her. Right now she likes you only a little better than Mortdh."

"Ouch."

"You broke her best friend's heart."

"I did not mean to."

Khiann rose to his feet and clapped him on his back. "When you find Gulan, you must have a heart-to-heart talk with her, and tell her what you told me about your family. Maybe it will take the sting out of what she perceives as your rejection."

"I will do my best."

Pulling Esag into a quick embrace, Khiann clapped his back again. "Good luck."

ANNANI

"My lady, Tula and her mother are here to see you," the guard informed Annani.

As per Gulan's request, she had invited Tula for an interview to take her sister's position as Annani's personal maid.

Twelve seemed so young, but then Gulan had been even younger when she started working for Annani. Except, she had been a little girl herself and had seen no wrong in that.

Now, Annani wondered if it had been right. Though in Gulan's case, they had attended school together, as well as studied with Annani's tutor.

Perhaps Annani could arrange that for Tula. The old tyrant was probably still looking for a new student to terrorize.

Good luck with that. Annani smirked. Tula would not let anyone intimidate her.

"Tell them I will be out in a moment." Annani wanted to talk to the girl alone, but she did not wish to offend the mother by having the guard admit only Tula.

"Yes, my lady." The immortal bowed.

Having her own reception chamber, including an antechamber for those who were waiting to see her, still felt odd. But now that she had interviews and meetings with the palace staff to conduct, Annani could no longer do so in her private quarters.

It was part of growing up and assuming responsibilities.

As she stepped out into the antechamber, both Tula and her mother pushed to their feet and bowed.

"Thank you for bringing Tula to the palace," she told the mother. "Is it okay if I talk to her alone?"

"Of course, my lady." The woman bowed again.

"Come, Tula." Annani waved the girl inside and closed the door behind her.

"Do you know where Gulan went, my lady?" Tula asked, her pointy little chin quivering.

Annani patted her shoulder. "I do not. But Esag is going to look for her."

Lifting her quivering chin, Tula stomped her foot. "It is all his fault. You should send someone else to look for her, not that stupid Esag." The girl crossed her arms over her budding breasts. "You should send warriors. Many of them."

As Tula's eyes blazed with anger, the inner light reminded Annani that as small as the girl was, she had already gone through her transition. When the start of her monthly cycle had signaled the onset of puberty, her parents had arranged for a transitioned boy to induce her transformation. According to Gulan, Tula had not waited for the boy to kiss her and had kissed him first.

Good for her.

Not getting a kiss during her transition ceremony had

been a sore point with Gulan. Tula had probably feared the same would happen to her and had taken the initiative.

She was a feisty little sprite.

"Gulan is an adult, and she is free to do as she pleases. I cannot send warriors after her to apprehend her like a criminal. Esag, on the other hand, has a chance of convincing her to come back willingly."

With a sigh, Tula plopped onto a chair. "She is not going to listen to him."

"I hope she does." Annani sat next to the girl. "I cannot think of anyone else who can persuade her that she is making a mistake."

"I can." Tula lifted her chin. "I will go with Esag, and I will make his life so miserable that he is going to regret every little hurt he caused Gulan."

Annani chuckled. "I bet you would. But that is not going to happen. In her note, Gulan asked me to hire you in her place because your family needs the income."

Tula lowered her chin and pouted. "I know. She left us a note too, saying the same thing."

Annani perked up. "Did she leave any hints as to where she was going?"

"Nope. All she wrote was how much she loved us all and that one day when her pain faded she was going to come back home. Until then, I was to take her place in your service."

"That is a shame. But it is not as if she could just go anywhere. Khiann and I think that she went north to Mortdh's stronghold."

Tula gasped. "Why would she do a stupid thing like that?"

"Where else could she go? There are no immortal settlements anywhere else."

A deep frown wrinkling her forehead, Tula brought her thumb to her mouth and started chewing on the nail. "Lady Areana is going up north, right? Did she leave yet?"

"No, she leaves the day after tomorrow. Why?"

"Maybe I can be her maid and go with her? If Gulan is there, I can convince her to go home, and the next time Areana comes for a visit she can bring us with her and leave us here."

This was not an entirely bad idea, except for the girls' poor parents who would be all alone, and for the unstable environment at Mortdh's stronghold. No one really knew what was going on up there, but since the immortals residing in his territory seemed loyal to him, he must have been treating them at least decently.

Or perhaps he was keeping them prisoner and not allowing them to visit and share their horror stories, or threatening them with retribution if they dared to tarnish his reputation.

Anything was possible.

"You should talk it over with your parents. If they agree, I will not try to stop you. But you should know that it is very different up there. Women are not treated with respect."

Tula rolled her eyes. "Duh, that is why I want Gulan to come back. It is crazy for a woman to go there willingly. I feel sorry for poor Lady Areana. She is so nice."

"Yes, I feel the same. I will forever be grateful for her sacrifice."

Her legs swinging back and forth, Tula leaned forward. "If Areana pays me as well as you paid Gulan, and the wages are sent to my parents, they will have no problem with letting me go after my sister."

"Are you sure?"

"I am sure. Can you ask Lady Areana if she is willing to take me and how much she can pay me?"

Annani choked down a chuckle. Tula was so different from Gulan. She was gutsy and direct, to the point of being rude. Hopefully, gentle Areana would have no problem employing the outspoken sprite.

"The palace will pay your wages in Areana's name. So you can assure them in that respect. But you still need to talk to Areana and see if she is willing to hire you. I will write a recommendation for you and explain the situation."

Tula jumped down from her chair, knelt in front of Annani, and clasped her hands. "Thank you! You are the kindest goddess ever." She kissed the back of one hand and then the other.

Annani pulled her up. "You are being silly, Tula. Go back to the antechamber and wait with your mother while I write the note."

"Thank you, my lady. You are the best." The girl ran out to share her exciting news.

When Annani was done, she called for both the girl and her mother.

"Here is the note to Lady Areana." She handed Tula the small scroll she had affixed with the royal seal, and then turned to the mother. "It is up to you and Tula's father to decide whether she can go or not. Personally, I think it is risky, and I would have preferred for her to stay here and serve as my maid. It is Tula's wish to follow her sister and try to convince her to come back. I want to make sure you understand that no one is expecting you to do anything you do not feel comfortable with."

The mother bowed her head. "I understand. Thank you, my lady. You are most kind."

"Lady Areana leaves the day after tomorrow. I suggest

that you take the rest of the day to think it over, and whether you decide to let Tula go or not, come back and let me know so I can inform my sister whether or not to expect you tomorrow."

ESAG

"*E*sag, this is Roven and that is Davuh." Khiann introduced the two warriors. "And this is Esag, my squire, who is going to lead the search for Gulan."

Esag clasped Roven's hand and then Davuh's. "We have a long journey ahead of us."

The two did not seem bothered. "We are glad to help," Davuh said.

Esag had no doubt. Khiann had told him that Annani had promised the two a generous bonus if they found Gulan. The men were highly motivated to succeed.

"Where do we start?" Roven asked.

While packing for the journey, Esag had formulated a plan. "First, we are going to check with all the merchant houses if a caravan of theirs headed out today. Then we are going to choose which one to follow." He mounted his horse and waited for the men to do the same.

Other than the horses they were riding, they were taking with them three more—one for Gulan, if and when they found her, and the other two to carry supplies for the long journey.

If it turned out to be long.

Esag still suspected that Gulan was hiding somewhere in the city, and he had persuaded Khiann to send guards to search for her.

"Did you hear back from Lady Areana?" he asked Khiann.

"Not yet. I sent her a message to check all her trunks, but I doubt any are big enough for Gulan to fit in."

"I will stop by before we hit the road. Can you send a messenger and check with her?"

"I will."

"Thanks."

It took them nearly two hours to visit all the merchant houses, and what they found out was that three caravans had left early that morning and another one was scheduled to leave the next day. The morning ones had gone in three directions. One had headed to Mortdh's territory, the other one had gone west for Kemet, and the third one had headed east. The one leaving tomorrow was only going to nearby cities.

"I say we follow the one going to Harappa," Esag said.

Davuh lifted a brow. "Why Harappa?"

"Because it was the last one to leave. We can catch up to it the fastest. If she is not there, we will reverse directions and go west."

"Why not north?" Roven asked. "Mortdh's territory is the obvious choice."

"For a male. Not for a female. Besides, Lady Areana is heading there. If she finds Gulan, she will send us a message. If we ride hard, we can catch up with the caravan in about three hours. If she is not there, we ride back, exchange horses for fresh ones, and ride west."

Davuh chuckled. "Maybe by the time we come back to

exchange horses, Lady Areana will have found Gulan hiding in one of her travel trunks."

Catching up to the eastbound caravan ended up taking four hours instead of three, and then they had to waste another half an hour searching all the wagons in case Gulan was hiding in one of the trunks.

"I told you Princess Annani's maid was not here," the irate caravan master huffed. "Can we leave now?"

"I am sorry for the delay, but Princess Annani is very worried about her maid. We have orders to check every caravan that left the city today." Esag rerolled the scroll with Annani's search orders and put it in his pocket. "Safe travels."

The caravan master nodded. "Good luck finding the girl."

"We cannot push the horses on the way back," Roven said. "By the time we get back to the city it is going to be too dark to head out west."

Esag was well aware of the fact. Chasing the wrong caravan had cost them a day. On the other hand, the caravan also had to stop for the night. "We will head out at first light tomorrow."

"It will take us several days to catch up to it," Roven said.

"Tell me something I do not know."

15

AREANA

*I*t was time.

The six weeks of waiting for Annani and Khiann's joining ceremony had seemed like such a long time, but they had flown by in a blur of preparations.

Standing in her front yard, Areana watched as the soldiers her father had assigned to her loaded her belongings onto the wagons.

That was what her life had amounted to—a few trunks filled with clothes and other necessities as well as a few personal mementos. The house she was leaving behind was the only thing that had given her a small measure of comfort throughout her grief. It was the only place where she had felt safe and where she had done what she could to help others.

It was so hard to say goodbye.

"Everything is ready, Lady Areana," the unit's captain said as the last trunk was loaded. "Would you like to check that all of your belongings are accounted for?"

"Yes, I should. Thank you."

"They are all there," Tula said. "I already counted them.

The trunks are in that one." She pointed to the second wagon. "And the other supplies are in the third, fourth and fifth."

The first wagon was fancier, its interior designed as a luxurious carriage to provide comfortable transport for Areana and Tula.

After hiring the girl, she had decided not to take any additional maids with her. Tula could take care of her personal needs, and Areana had no problem with eating whatever the soldiers' cook prepared.

Twelve immortal warriors were accompanying her on her journey, and they brought with them a human cook to prepare their meals, four squires to take care of the animals and the daily tent building and dismantling, and five human wagon drivers.

They were going to make several stops on the way and purchase fresh supplies, but most of it was coming with them in the three wagons.

With a heavy sigh, Areana walked back inside to say goodbye to her staff.

"We are going to miss you so much, my lady." Her maid sniffled.

"And I you." Areana hugged her briefly before moving on to the next one.

The last was the immortal she had hired to manage her charity. "If you run into any trouble, you can turn to Princess Annani for help."

"Yes, I know. You have told me so already, my lady. You have nothing to worry about. Everything is going to run as smoothly as it did under your care."

"Yes, well, just in case something comes up, I want you to have someone to turn to, and Princess Annani promised to help in any way she could."

Annani had also promised to come say goodbye, but

she was running late. Perhaps she was waiting for Ahn to join her?

Even after all the disappointments Areana had endured from her father, she could not help but wish he would surprise her and come to see her off. Did she not deserve a little bit of courtesy for her sacrifice? A little attention from her sire?

After all, she had given up what little pleasure she still derived from life to please him.

As she waited for her sister to arrive, Areana took a long stroll through her house, committing every detail to memory. If Mortdh allowed her to come back for visits, she would get to enjoy her home from time to time, but Areana had a feeling that she was never going to see it again.

Perhaps she saw everything through darkened goggles because her spirits were so low.

Lower than usual even for her.

As someone who had been depressed for decades, she should not have felt worse for leaving her home, and yet she did.

The home she had shared with Ahnon was the last part of him she had clung to, and now she was leaving even that behind.

"Lady Areana." Tula rushed after her. "I saw Princess Annani's carriage pulling up in front of the house. You should come out."

Areana forced a smile. "Of course."

The last spark of hope had just been snuffed out. Ahn was not coming after all.

16

NAVUH

*A*reana's convoy had left ten days ago, and with each passing day, Navuh's concern for her intensified.

According to his spies, she had twelve of Ahn's best palace guards accompanying her, along with several squires, a cook, and a maid. Three wagons and twelve warriors on horseback should be enough to deter bandits, and yet he knew of even larger caravans that had been attacked.

Regrettably, he had no way of spying on her until she reached her first populated stop. In the meantime, he was in the dark, and anxiety was not a feeling Navuh was comfortable with.

He did not get anxious often.

Even his father's insanity, which posed the greatest threat to Navuh, had a pattern he could predict with reasonable accuracy. For everything else, he had contingencies and safeguards in place that allowed him to sleep well at night.

Until Areana.

Since he had seen her sad, pleading eyes in Ahn's throne room, he had not had a moment's peace.

It was not that he was in love with her. Navuh was too smart to allow himself to have strong feelings for anyone. But once he had decided she was his, Areana had become his responsibility, and he had to check up on her and make sure she was safe.

Besides, he needed more time.

Mortdh did not have any upcoming travel plans that required him to use the flyer. Until he did, Navuh would have to stall for time. He had to find Areana and tell her to slow down, making as many rest stops on the way as was reasonable for a pampered goddess unused to the road's harsh conditions.

Which meant many days of rest interspersed with a few days of travel. She could drag out the journey for up to three moon cycles.

The two warriors stationed outside his father's door bowed to Navuh as he neared.

A brief moment passed as one of the guards went in and announced him, then returned and opened the way. "Lord Mortdh will see you now."

"Thank you."

He entered the room and bowed. "Good afternoon, Father. May I have a word with you?"

Mortdh waved the servants away, then put a silencing shroud around the chamber. "What news do you bring me, son?"

"Areana's convoy left ten days ago, accompanied by twelve of Ahn's best men. I thought I could stop by under the pretext of checking up on her and ask the men some questions. We do not have any spies inside Ahn's palace guard."

Mortdh eyed him suspiciously. "They are not going to tell you anything of importance."

Navuh smirked. "I have my ways to get people to talk."

"That you do. It often astounds me what information you manage to gather. What is your secret? Do you have your own spy network?"

"I do not." Navuh spread his arms wide. "All I have are my charm and charisma."

It was not entirely a lie. He did not have his own spies, but Mortdh's extensive network reported to Navuh first, and if he wanted additional information without his father knowing about it, all he had to do was ask.

Except, this was not his only secret. He had another method of gathering information, but his father was too arrogant to suspect it. Mortdh would have found it inconceivable that his lowly immortal son should possess a godly skill.

"What do you hope to learn?" Mortdh asked.

"Whatever new information I can get is better than none. We do not even know the exact number of warriors Ahn employs. Other than that, I want to know how many hours a day they train, and if they use their chariots only to transport officers or do they train to use them in battle." He saved the most tantalizing bit for last. "I can also find out how many guards in civilian garb Ahn has assigned to follow the usurper around."

"Yes, this would be most useful information. I assume you came to me because you wish to borrow the flyer?"

"Just for tonight. I will find their encampment, spend a few hours coaxing information out of the warriors, and come back."

"All right." Mortdh waved a dismissive hand. "Just do not bring the widow back with you, not even if she complains about the hardships of the road."

"I have no intention of doing so. Paying her a visit, but not taking her with me, will further humiliate Ahn."

Smoothing his hand over his short beard, Mortdh nodded. "I like the way you think, son."

"Thank you, Father." Navuh bowed. "I will report to you on the morrow."

As Navuh counted the hours until nightfall, the excitement he felt bubbling up in his chest was most disconcerting. It was true that he had desired the fair goddess since he was a young boy, and it was also true that mating Ahn's daughter would no doubt raise his profile in the eyes of the other gods, but that did not mean he had to lose his head over her.

Literally or figuratively.

After all, she was just a woman, and not his truelove mate.

And yet, he could not remember being so excited about anything since he had reached adulthood. Even his nomination as Mortdh's successor and second-in-command, a position he had worked long and hard for, had not shaken his rock-solid equilibrium as much as the prospect of seeing Areana and her possible seduction.

Navuh's harem was not as big as Mortdh's, but he had a decent selection of immortal beauties to choose from, all of whom wanted nothing more than to please him in any way they could.

But none of them was a goddess.

Except, he would be lying to himself if he believed even for a moment that this was the only reason he wanted Areana. There was something about her that was absent even in other goddesses.

She was pure.

Maybe that was why his father's rude comment about her being used goods had enraged Navuh so. She had been with only one male, her mate, and since his death, she had not even looked in the direction of another male.

However, her purity was not only about her chaste existence. Areana was good through and through. She did not have even one mean or selfish bone in her body. She would not hurt a fly. Everything Areana did was to help others without expecting anything in return.

She was his exact opposite. The light to his darkness.

When Navuh treated others well, it was because he wanted their loyalty, and if he gave out praise and encouragement it was for the same reason. He did not believe in giving for the sake of charity. When he rewarded people for a job well done, it was so they would do even better the next time.

Every move was calculated to promote his own agenda.

17

AREANA

A wet washrag in hand, Areana dabbed at her sweaty neck, then dripped a little more water on it and dabbed at her forehead.

The wagon's canopy and sides had to remain closed to shield her sensitive eyes and skin from the blazing sun, which meant nearly suffocating in the stifling heat.

She was sweaty, sticky, and much more miserable than usual.

Traveling through the day was more challenging than she had expected, but unfortunately, the animals pulling the wagons and her escort's horses could not travel in the dark.

Tula, who as an immortal did not suffer from the same sensitivity to the sun, sat up front with the wagon driver, chatting his head off.

The old human did not seem to mind.

In fact, the only thing keeping Areana from going insane was listening to his stories about the many adventures he had had on the caravan routes and the distant cities he had visited.

Aside from the unbearable heat, getting bumped around the wagon was no fun either.

Maybe tomorrow she would put her protective goggles on, cover her face with a scarf, and go sit up front with Tula and the wagon driver.

Ugh. As if the caravan master would agree to that. Transporting a goddess was making everyone jumpy, and he preferred her to stay out of sight.

Areana could argue that her glow was not as noticeable during the day, and that with her hair covered no one could see its tell-tale pallidity, but she had a feeling the guy was just going to shake his head, apologize profusely for the inconvenience, and tell her to stay hidden inside the wagon.

But even as torturous as the journey was, Areana was in no hurry for it to end. Nothing good was awaiting her at her final destination.

Except for maybe a bath.

Fates, how she wished to immerse herself in water and wash the sweat and grime off. Even a cold spring would do. In fact, it would be preferable to a hot bath.

When the wagon finally stopped, Tula lifted the fabric flap and offered Areana a hand. "How are you holding up, my lady?"

"As well as can be expected." She took the girl's hand and stepped out of the wagon.

It was still hot outside, but the sun was setting, and with it the heat would give way to the night's chill. The desert climate was much more extreme than that of the coastal city she had come from.

Thank the merciful Fates.

The cool nights were a most welcome respite.

"Would you like to go on a short stroll while the men put up the tents?" Tula asked.

"That would be lovely."

After spending all day in the swaying wagon, her first few steps were wobbly, but so were Tula's.

"We look like a couple of sailors." The girl giggled.

"Now that you mention it, I do not know why the captain did not plan on going west and using a boat for at least part of the journey. I am sure it would have been more pleasant."

Tula nodded. "Not as hot."

"We could have gone swimming in the sea."

"I do not know how to swim, my lady. Do you?"

"Yes, I do. And I would have taught you. It is quite fun." The last time Areana had gone swimming was with Ahnon. It was a pleasant memory of youth and hope and happier times. She sighed. "It has been many years since I did anything fun."

Tula cast her a questioning glance. "Why? You are a goddess, and you can do as you please."

"After my mate was taken away from me, I lost the will to do fun things."

Looking down at her feet, Tula was quiet for a couple of moments. "I know you are sad, my lady. But maybe if you did more fun stuff, you would not be as sad."

Simple truth. And yet there was nothing simple about the crippling effects of grief. It would be difficult for a young girl like Tula to understand, and Areana did not feel like explaining. Why weigh down those slender shoulders with a burden that was not hers?

"What do you like to do for fun, Tula?"

The girl smirked. "I like to dress up and pretend that I am a high-born lady. But not by myself, I like to do it with my friends." The corners of her lips reversed directions. "Now that I am all grown up and have work and responsibilities, I guess I will not be doing that anymore."

Areana ruffled her hair. "You are far from grown up, Tula. When we get to Mortdh's palace, I promise to play dress up with you until you find new friends to play with."

Her jaw slack, Tula lifted a pair of wide eyes to Areana. "But you are a goddess! There is no one higher than that. What would you dress up as?"

Good question. "I can dress up as a servant, and you will be the lady."

Gasping, Tula shook her head. "Oh, no, I cannot do that, my lady."

"Why not? I heard that my sister dressed as a commoner to go see Khiann." She leaned to whisper in Tula's ear. "And she told me that you were an accomplice, and so was your sister."

"That was different. Annani dressed up as a commoner, not a servant, and she did not serve us. We were still the ones serving her."

"You wore her dress and pretended to be her."

"But no one saw me. I just stayed in her bed and hid under the covers in case someone entered her room to check up on her. That was all."

Areana was about to retort when a distant hum had her lifting her eyes to the sky. "Did you hear that?"

Tula looked up. "Hear what?"

"I think it is a flying boat."

Taking hold of Areana's elbow, Tula urged, "Please, my lady. Let us go back. What if it is Lord Mortdh coming to take you?"

NAVUH

*W*hile piloting the flyer, Navuh had a breakthrough—a solution to the problem of getting rid of Mortdh that was so elegant and so obvious that he wondered why he had not thought of it before.

The first and most challenging step of the plan was goading Mortdh into committing Khiann's murder himself, instead of sending out assassins to do the deed for him.

If reliable witnesses reported the crime to Ahn, Mortdh would be tried for murder and sentenced to entombment, and Navuh would have no problem arranging that.

The beauty of this plan was that not even a speck of blame would land on him, and as his father's official successor, Navuh would take over the rule of the northern province without anyone batting an eyelid.

Clean and easy, except for the first part. That and Khiann actually leaving the safety of the city walls anytime soon. Hopefully, before Areana's arrival at court.

Playing on Mortdh's injured pride, Navuh would convince him that the only way to restore his honor was for the usurper to die by his hand. He would suggest that a rumor, which supposedly could not be proven, would be deliberately spread so everyone would know who had done it. As a warning to others, it was of crucial importance to show that no one took what was Mortdh's and lived to enjoy it.

An assassination could achieve similar goals, but it lacked the poetic justice myths were made of. Hopefully, his hotheaded and prideful father would take the bait.

Spotting Areana's camp, Navuh started his descent toward a stretch of flat desert land. The small flyer did not require much of a runway and could land almost vertically, but upon landing it would stir up a cloud of sand. Areana would not appreciate him messing up her campsite.

Her guards did not seem troubled by his arrival, which was not surprising. There were only four flying boats that could still take to the air, and all four belonged to the royal family. Three of them were Ahn's, but Mortdh's brother Toven was always using one of them for his exploratory expeditions, and the fourth was Mortdh's. None of them posed a threat to their lady.

At least in theory.

"Lord Navuh." The captain bowed respectfully. "We were not expecting you."

"I was sent to check up on Lady Areana's safety and well-being."

"Of course." The captain bowed again. "I will let the lady know that you are here to see her." He turned on his heel and strode toward the largest tent.

The flyer did not make much noise, but it should have been enough for the goddess to know that he was coming. Except, she probably expected Mortdh. Or maybe even her father. Although that would have been foolish of her. Ahn would not have bothered, and Mortdh would not have flown in without a squadron of his warriors arriving beforehand to receive him.

After announcing Navuh, the captain emerged from Areana's tent and bowed again. "The lady will see you now."

"Thank you." Navuh rewarded the man with a smile.

Later, after he was done with the goddess, he was going to ask the captain a few questions. It would do no harm to have him positively disposed towards him.

"What a lovely surprise." Areana rose to her feet and walked toward him. "I did not expect to see you until I arrived at court."

She was flushed, her face reddened either from sun exposure or excitement at seeing him.

Unfortunately, it must have been the former and not the latter, since he could detect no scent of arousal. For some reason, though, she smelled of embarrassment. Was she worried about her haggard appearance?

She was even more beautiful to him like this.

Her sweat-slicked skin evoked images of her perspiring from an entirely different kind of heat. And if that was not enough, the way her dress clung damply to her body further fueled his lustful musings.

Get a hold of yourself.

"I was worried." Navuh strode toward Areana and took her delicate hand. "I had to check up on you and see that you were safe." He brought it up to his lips and kissed the back of it lightly.

Usually, his manners were impeccable, but as he resisted the strange impulse to lick the sweat off her hand and find out if she tasted sweet, Navuh held on for a moment longer than acceptable.

Her heartbeat accelerating, Areana pulled her hand away just in time. "That is very kind of you. But as you can see, I am perfectly fine." She chuckled nervously. "Or as fine as could be expected after ten days without a proper bath."

The tent flap lifting had him turn his head and glare at the intruder—a young girl holding a water jug and a stack of washing cloths.

"Excuse me." She brushed by Navuh as if he was a nobody and rushed to her lady's side. "I did not know you had company, my lady." As the lie left her lips, the girl looked askance at Navuh.

Gutsy little thing. Did she not know who he was?

Areana cast him an apologetic glance, then turned to her maid. "Thank you, Tula. You can leave everything behind the privacy screen."

The girl did as she was told, then came back and gave Navuh a thorough once-over. "You are not Lord Mortdh."

If he were, she would have been in big trouble for her disrespectful attitude. Luckily for her, Navuh was more forgiving than his father. Besides, he needed to leave a good impression on Areana. "No, little girl. I am his son, Lord Navuh."

She pursed her lips. "Oh."

"You may leave us, Tula," Areana said more sternly.

The girl offered her a little curtsy. "If you need me, my lady, I will be outside with the wagon drivers." She threw one last curious glance at Navuh before lifting the tent flap. "Should I bring dinner in when it is ready?"

"Yes, please. And tell the cook I have an important guest."

"As you wish, my lady." The girl let the flap drop behind her.

Areana waited a moment before waving her hand at a floor cushion. "Please, take a seat, Lord Navuh."

He bowed. "After you, Lady Areana."

Rearranging the folds of her skirt, Areana tucked her pale legs under her. "I apologize for my young maid. She has just started working for me and does not know the proper etiquette yet."

"Obviously." He sat on the cushion she had indicated. "Make sure to teach her before she arrives at my father's court. He is not as forgiving as I."

Areana tried and failed to suppress a grimace. "I hope I will manage to do so in the time I have." She leaned and picked up a pitcher. "May I offer you water?"

"Yes, please."

She poured it into two goblets and handed him one.

As he took it from her, Navuh intentionally brushed his fingers over hers, curious to see if her heartbeat would accelerate again.

It did.

Areana was definitely not indifferent to him.

If he played his hand well, before he left her he might coax a kiss out of the shy beauty.

Maybe even more.

The thought amused him. It had been ages since he had played the seduction game. Having all the females he could want or handle at his beck and call, he had not expected to be doing any wooing.

And yet, here he was, dusting off his rusty flirting skills to seduce the fairest of goddesses.

AREANA

avuh, a mere immortal, was succeeding where several gods had tried and failed. He was getting under Areana's skin, awakening sensations that had lain dormant for decades.

He was like no one else she had ever met.

Dark and dangerous, he was nonetheless polite to a fault, but without the overdone mannerisms many of the male gods displayed.

Their politeness was a sham, meant to show off their superior upbringing and polished social etiquette. But under that thin layer of civility, most were pompous and condescending—their feelings of superiority over a weak goddess like Areana transparent.

Navuh, on the other hand, seemed to treat her with genuine respect and appreciation. Was it because he was only an immortal and therefore felt inferior to her?

It would have been a reasonable assumption if she had not witnessed him showing much less respect to Ahn, the most powerful of the gods.

But why?

Other than being Ahn's daughter, a fact her father had treated like a dirty secret, Areana was at the very bottom of the godly hierarchy.

Maybe Navuh treated her with respect because she was Mortdh's intended?

That would have been a reasonable explanation as well, except for the way Navuh's eyes smoldered when he looked at her, and the way the potency of his male scent flared in her presence.

Navuh wanted her for himself.

And for the first time since Ahnon's death, the thought of someone lusting after her excited Areana rather than disturbed her.

Navuh put his goblet down and pinned her with his unnerving intense gaze. "You must be wondering why I did not offer to take you back with me in the flyer."

The thought had crossed her mind, but she was grateful he had not made the offer. As much as she hated the long land journey, taking to the skies terrified her.

"Is it a two-person vehicle?"

"It can accommodate up to four average-sized adults if no additional weight is added—meaning no luggage. I could have taken you and your little maid, but there is a good reason why I am not offering to. My father is in a foul mood, and it would be better for you to arrive later rather than sooner."

At the mention of the hateful god, Areana's gut twisted painfully. "Is it because of me? Is he angry that I stayed for my sister's joining ceremony?"

Navuh chuckled. "No, Lady Areana, it is not because of you. He does not even mention you."

That was somewhat offensive, but Areana could live with that. Being the focus of Mortdh's attention was not a good thing.

"I would love to follow your advice and tarry for as long as I can, but my father's men have a schedule to keep. Besides, I do not know how much longer I can tolerate the insufferable heat and the bumpy wagon."

Navuh smiled. "This is the best excuse for you to cut west toward the sea and stop for rests in the coastal cities along the way. The larger ones have inns with rooms for rent, where you can have a proper bath and have your garments laundered."

Areana sighed. "That sounds heavenly."

"And very reasonable. A goddess, who is used to a life of luxury, would naturally tire of the road and would want to make frequent stops, resting for several days each time. Which brings me to the subject of a budget. I am sure your provisions are not sufficient for additional days of travel." He pulled a hefty pouch out of his pocket.

As her cheeks heated in embarrassment, Areana lifted a hand to stop him and shook her head. "Please put it away, Lord Navuh. I am not short of funds." Ahn had provided her with plenty.

"I am sure of that. But, please, take it anyway." He leaned over and put the pouch next to Areana's pillow. "Treat it as an emergency fund in case something unforeseen comes up. If you wish, you can return it when you arrive. But in the meantime, I will sleep better knowing you are not going to run out of money."

By the determined expression on his face, Navuh was not going to listen to any further arguments. Besides, Areana did not like confrontations, and this was starting to feel like one.

"If it makes you sleep better, I will accept it as a temporary loan, and upon my arrival, I will return every last coin."

A suggestive smirk lifting one corner of his perfect

mouth, Navuh leaned toward her. "It would please me greatly if you used the money to pamper yourself." His voice had deepened.

With the polite mask dropped, all that was left was a lustful predator regarding her as if she was a sumptuous meal.

As his masculine scent enveloped her in a cloud of temptation, a heat of a different kind rushed through Areana's body.

"My lady?" Tula lifted the tent flap. "Dinner is ready. Should I bring it in?"

"Yes, please." Areana was grateful for the timely interruption.

Schooling her features, she smiled apologetically at Navuh. "I hope you do not mind the simple meal. I thought it would be a waste to bring my own cook on the journey." The truth was that she did not want to bring any females to Mortdh's territory, and the only reason she had taken Tula was that the girl had begged her to.

The polite mask back in place, Navuh inclined his head. "Not at all. I am not a finicky eater."

His acting ability was impressive. Then again, Navuh was a politician and Mortdh's successor. In his situation, excellent acting skills were necessary for survival.

As Tula entered with a large tray in her hands, the cook followed timidly with another.

Once the two of them were done setting the low table, the human scurried away, but Tula remained.

"Can you ask Lord Navuh about my sister?" she whispered loudly in Areana's ear, and then looked at Navuh as if expecting him to answer.

"Who is your sister, little girl?"

"My name is Tula." She looked at him pointedly. "Gulan is my sister. She was Princess Annani's maid, but she ran away because she was brokenhearted over a stupid guy." Tula paused to take a breath and lifted her hand way above her head. "Gulan is really tall, nearly as tall as you, my lord. She is hard to miss."

To his credit, Navuh smiled instead of getting angry at Tula for addressing him as if he were her friend. "I did not see anyone who matches your description."

"Oh." Tula's chin dropped all the way down to her chest. "How stupid of me. Gulan is probably still on the road."

Areana patted her arm. "That is right. Gulan left the morning after the ceremony and is traveling with a caravan. Many days will pass before she reaches the Northern Territory."

Navuh cleared his throat and looked at Tula, indicating that he wanted her to leave.

Disappointed, the girl curtsied. "I will be out with the drivers if you need me, my lady."

When the tent flap fluttered into place, Areana offered Navuh an apologetic smile. "This is why I brought Tula with me instead of a more experienced maid. She wants to find her sister and persuade her to come home."

"What made her think that her sister headed north?"

"Where else would a lone immortal female go if she wanted to disappear?"

Navuh shrugged. "Anywhere, really. Immortals can pretend to be human and live among them. Provided they get up and move to a new place every decade or so, no one needs to know that they are not like everyone else."

NAVUH

*A*reana had merely nibbled on the food, and not because it was unpalatable. For road rations, it was not bad.

"May I ask you a few questions about your father's court?" she asked.

So that was what had been troubling her. "Go ahead."

Lifting a cloth napkin, she twisted it between her slender fingers. "I have heard that Mortdh has a large harem with many concubines and many children."

"This is true." Except that the children were not really Mortdh's, but then it was a secret no one was supposed to know, including Navuh.

"Am I going to live in that harem?"

"Most likely."

Not if he could help it. By the time Areana arrived at court, Mortdh would hopefully be in the council's custody.

His father's harem, though, would have to go through some changes. Up until Areana had mentioned it, Navuh had not given it much thought. He should start formulating a plan for repurposing it.

The females would enter Navuh's version of a breeding program, which was going to produce significantly more children than it currently was.

Navuh would keep building the army, filling its ranks with as many immortal warriors as possible.

Lowering her eyes, Areana let out a sigh. "I was afraid of that."

He wished he could tell her that she had nothing to worry about, but he could not trust her with his secret plans. No one could ever know that he was responsible for orchestrating Mortdh's demise.

Not now. Not ever.

"You will no doubt be granted your own suite of rooms. Besides, the harem is not a bad place to live in. It's quite luxurious, and the women are mostly friendly. If you like children, you will be glad to know that there are many of them running around the place."

That brought a smile to her lips. "I love children. And since I am pretty sure Mortdh will forget all about me, I will at least have the other women for company." She sighed. "I do not know how they can tolerate being treated like breeding stock. I guess none of them love him."

Navuh chuckled. "Probably not."

His father was not an easy male to love, and he was wise enough to treat all the women with the same indifference. If he paid one more attention than the others, her life would become intolerable. Jealousy could cause severe problems in a harem.

Mortdh was obsessed with proving his fertility. His harem was full of immortal females that he was trying to impregnate, but without much success.

Navuh was not supposed to know, but Mortdh had fathered only one son—him. His other so-called children had been the result of affairs between his concubines and his harem guards and servants. Since he did not care for any of the women and his main goal was to appear fruitful and potent and to claim to have fathered as many children as possible, Mortdh pretended not to know.

That was another lesson Navuh had learned from his father, except he implemented it on a much smaller scale and with much more discrimination. His harem was tiny in comparison to his father's, and the males he employed in its service were all intelligent and shared at least some of his features. If he were to claim the children as his own, he wanted them to have brains and to look like him. So far, his harem had produced only one child. Thankfully, it was a boy who looked enough like Navuh to avoid suspicion.

"It is good that I am not looking forward to a romantic relationship with Mortdh," Areana said. "There can be no romantic love connection between more than two people."

"That is true."

Which meant if Navuh wanted Areana to be his, he would have to either dispense with his harem or let her in on his secret. He could promise her never to touch the other females and hope she would be all right with the arrangement.

Areana might give him a son one day, but as a goddess, her chances of conceiving were not good. In the meantime, he wanted to claim more children as his own and groom them for positions of power in his future government.

A good ruler needed capable people he could delegate tasks to.

"I am glad you see things my way. I was afraid you'd share your father's opinion."

Was that a hint?

Was Areana admitting her interest in him?

It was time to find out. "Would you like to join me for a

stroll outside?" He patted his middle. "I overate, and I could use a walk."

"I would love to, but I do not think the captain would like me to leave the camp area."

Navuh pushed to his feet and offered Areana a hand up. "Leave it to me. I will handle him."

With a smile, she put her small hand in his. As he pulled her up, Navuh wished he could bring her closer to him and kiss her senseless.

Patience.

They were surrounded by immortals with superior hearing. The only one who could cast a silencing shroud to block them out was the goddess, and he could not ask her to do so yet.

She needed to learn to trust him first. In order to accomplish that, however, he had to lead her away from the men and the nosy little maid, and woo her.

Except, the captain proved to be a stubborn man and not easily intimidated. "I will have four warriors follow at a respectful distance."

Navuh lifted a hand to stop any further resistance. "That will not be necessary." He imbued his voice with just a tiny thread of compulsion.

Hopefully, Areana did not notice.

As a goddess she might be able to use compulsion, but he doubted it. Not all gods possessed the ability, and using it on other gods was frowned upon.

As far as he knew, Navuh was the only immortal who had been born with the unique talent. Ever since he had first discovered the ability, he had kept it a secret from all. Not only did it give him a tremendous advantage over other immortals, but it also made him immune to it, which meant that Mortdh could not compel him to do as he pleased.

The Fates had seen fit to grant him this one-of-a-kind skill for a reason, and Navuh was not going to squander their gift by carelessly giving himself away.

"It will not be necessary," the captain parroted.

"Thank you. I promise to keep Lady Areana safe." Navuh put his hand on the small of Areana's back and led her away into the night.

"How did you do it?" she asked.

Putting on one of his most intimidating expressions, he turned to look at her. "Like this." He pointed to his face.

Surprising him, Areana giggled. "I see what you mean. That is one scary face. Still handsome, though." She threaded her arm through his.

Was she flirting with him?

And was he imagining it, or had her glow intensified?

It must have been an optical illusion. They had just left a well-illuminated tent, where her glow was not as noticeable. In the dark, her luminescence was much more evident. Except, a moment ago she did not glow as brightly. Did it flare up and dim according to her moods?

He had never heard of a god's or a goddess's glow reflecting their feelings. That would have been even more inconvenient than the emotional scents they were emitting. On the other hand, they had the ability to subdue it. Maybe when Areana was sad, she instinctively dimmed her natural illumination.

It was a hypothesis Navuh was most curious to examine. "Would you like me to show you the flyer?"

She shook her head. "I am terrified of air travel."

"We are not going to take off. I will not even turn the engine on."

"Then by all means. As long as it is on the ground and does not move, I am even willing to sit inside of it."

Perfect.

Away from the campsite and steeped in darkness, the flyer provided the privacy required for a secret kiss.

21

AREANA

*I*t had been a long while since Areana had taken part in a flirting game, but that did not mean she had forgotten how it was played.

Navuh was acting like a young boy luring a girl into a dark spot so he could steal a kiss.

She was playing along—just as she had done all those years ago when Ahnon had started courting her—pretending to be clueless as to his intentions.

Navuh was not Ahnon, though.

There was tangible darkness and danger in him. And yet, she did not think he was evil. But then she did not think Mortdh was evil either, just insane and misguided.

Except, that did not mean Mortdh was not a villain.

A villain was someone who did bad things, and it did not matter that he justified his evil deeds by making up some scenario that made sense only in his twisted mind.

Unlike Mortdh, however, Navuh was perfectly sane. Areana did not feel threatened by him. And it was not only because she was a goddess and he was an immortal, and she could overpower him by taking over his mind.

Maybe.

Navuh exuded power. It was possible that his mind was too strong even for a goddess to manipulate.

Or a god.

She had a feeling that Navuh had survived for as long as he had, and had risen to such a prominent position in Mortdh's court, because he was immune to mind manipulation.

Mortdh had many immortal sons, and yet he had chosen Navuh as his successor. He must have had a good reason to do so.

The way she saw it, Navuh liked her and wanted her to like him back, and he did not mean her harm.

Kissing him could be a very good idea.

He was very influential in Mortdh's court, and if she could influence the influencer, she would have a better foothold in her new and terrifying home. Having someone she could turn to for help would greatly reduce her anxiety.

Except, Areana was well aware that all of those good reasons were not why she was there, walking with Navuh toward his vehicle and tingling with anticipation.

Her intense craving for him had nothing to do with reason.

It was undeniable. If he did not kiss her tonight, she might do the unthinkable and kiss him first.

Shameful.

Maybe there was a limit to how long her body could tolerate the self-imposed abstinence, which was supposedly unnatural for a goddess.

But that was not it either. It was Navuh. No other male had succeeded in awakening her desires, and not for lack of effort. In comparison to others who had vied for her interest, Navuh had done very little.

Next to nothing, really.

A smoldering look, a brush of his fingers against hers, those should have done nothing for her. But there was one thing Navuh had done better than any of the gods who had come courting her after Ahnon's death.

When in her presence, he was giving her his undivided attention, and the singular intensity of that focus was what had broken through her shields.

"Here it is." Navuh pointed to the flyer.

It was painted black, and much smaller than she had imagined. Its body was only the size of a chariot, but its wings were long.

"Do the wings flap like those of a bird?"

"They move a little in the wind, but they do not flap. Do you want me to show you how they work?"

She eyed the vehicle suspiciously. "Do you have to turn the engine on for that?"

"Yes."

"Then I will pass."

"There is really nothing to fear. In fact, flying through the sky is quite exhilarating." He put his large hands on her waist and lifted her into the carriage, then leaped in, using only one hand for leverage.

Show-off. Areana stifled a chuckle.

Wrapping his arms around her shoulders, he asked, "Are you comfortable?"

If he was asking about the seat, then yes, she was comfortable. His closeness, however, was anything but.

It was so long since she'd had a male pressed against her side, and not just any male, but Navuh, the most potent male she had ever met.

Areana chose honesty over convention. "No, I am not. How can I be comfortable with you so near?"

He misunderstood, taking his arm away and scooting sideways. "My apologies."

"No, that was not what I meant. I find your presence disturbing because…" the right words eluded her. Well, that was not true, she was just too much of a coward to say them. "Because I want you so much."

His arm returned, its weight on her shoulders both comforting and disturbing. "I want you too." His lips found the column of her neck, and he pressed a light kiss to it. "So soft." He kissed another spot. "I have never felt skin as smooth and as soft as yours."

She wanted to say something witty or seductive, but this time she really was lost for words. The sensations his soft kisses were evoking were too overwhelming.

"Did you know that your skin glows brighter when you get excited?" Navuh whispered in her ear, his warm breath fanning over the side of her face.

"I did not."

"Or maybe it glows brighter when you are happy?" He hooked a finger under her chin and turned her head to face him. "Are you happy to be with me, Areana?"

Happy was not the right word.

Hit by lightning was more like it, consumed by the inferno that was suddenly raging inside her, those were some of the images flitting through her head, but none of which she could verbalize.

The only words that came to her mind were 'take me right now.' Instead, she nodded as much as the finger under her chin allowed.

Slowly, as if he had all the time in the world, Navuh leaned closer until their lips finally touched.

Soft, his lips were so soft on hers, as if he was kissing a fragile flower petal, and not a resilient goddess. But even that barely-there touch was enough for the moan that had been seven decades in the making to escape Areana's throat.

22

NAVUH

*H*is Areana was not as timid as he had thought. Under that cool and righteous exterior, there was a lustful goddess with enough pent-up sexual frustration to light up the skies.

Moving his hand to the back of her head, he threaded his fingers through her pale hair and held her in place for a proper kiss.

As her lips parted in invitation, she rewarded him with another throaty moan.

Navuh's instinct was to conquer and plunder, but he held himself in check, flicking his tongue over her lush lips and getting a little taste of her.

So sweet.

Areana was so different from the immortal females he had bedded. There was nothing like it in the world. He was tasting the nectar of the gods.

As his tongue penetrated her mouth, Navuh pushed a hand under her bottom and lifted her onto his lap. But if he thought Areana would have a problem with his hard rod probing her behind, he had been very mistaken.

Another soft groan escaping her throat, she rubbed her bottom against his hardness and wrapped her arms around his neck. Then she kissed him back.

Dear merciful Fates.

He had not expected such fervor. A little more of this and he would strip her naked and plunge into her like a battering ram.

If she were anyone else, he would have not hesitated for another second, but this was the goddess he was planning on mating, and more than great sex was needed to win her heart—a heart that was still broken and in need of mending.

Except, it was easier said than done.

Navuh prided himself on his formidable willpower, but with Areana pressing her soft breasts against his chest and swiveling her hips in his lap, he was fighting a losing battle.

The hand with which he was supporting her back circled her ribcage as if it was acting on its own. The most he could do as far as getting permission was to force that impudent appendage to rest for a second under Areana's breast. When she showed no signs of displeasure, he released his hold and allowed the hand to cup the goddess's breast.

They both groaned in unison.

All calculation thrown to the wind, Navuh went with instinct and pinched her nipple through her dress. Not hard, but not softly either.

The sudden flare in the scent of her arousal proved that his instinct had been right. Areana did not want gentle.

Dear Fates, give me strength.

Right now Areana was as mindless with passion as he was, but he had a feeling she would not appreciate being taken in the cramped interior of Mortdh's flyer.

Mortdh's flyer!

Damnation. He had forgotten where they were. If they had sex there, Mortdh would smell it and execute Navuh, not because he cared about Areana and her chastity, but because it would be an unforgivable affront to his pride.

Holding her to him, he pressed his cheek to hers. "We must stop."

"Why?"

"Because this is my father's vehicle and he will smell the scent of our desire and figure out what we did in here."

"Donkey dung." Areana uttered a most unladylike curse. "We are so stupid. My guards must suspect what we are doing here, and they might talk—not maliciously, but people gossip. If word of this reaches Mortdh, we are both dead."

It was insane, but he liked that they shared a conspiracy. There was not much else he could share with Areana without putting himself and her at risk, but they had this stolen moment together.

"Do not worry about the guards. I will tell them to keep quiet."

"And you think they will listen to you? They do not answer to you or Mortdh, only to Ahn."

He was going to compel them to silence, but he could not tell her that. "They will keep their mouths shut if I tell them that your life depends on their discretion. I am sure your father would execute whoever talked and by doing so endangered your life."

Areana shifted to the other seat. "You overestimate my importance in my father's eyes. I am the embarrassment he wishes he had never fathered."

He knew that, and it angered him. "I am sure this is not so. You are beautiful, smart, and kind. Any father would be proud to call you a daughter. And if Ahn cannot see that, then he is more of a fool than I think he is."

Areana lifted a brow. "You think Ahn is a fool?"

It had been a slip of the tongue, but he had no problem owning up to it. "I think most gods are fools. Your father, my father, and all the other gods who do nothing but sit in their temples and accept offerings. Immortals outnumber them twenty or thirty to one, and this is only the beginning. Gods started mating with humans only about a hundred years ago. Imagine what will happen in another century and then another and another."

"Do you think the immortals will revolt?"

Yes, but again he could not share this with her. "As long as gods can take control of immortal and human minds, a revolt is not likely. It would be quashed before it even began."

Except, he was training an army to block their minds against godly manipulation. Mortdh thought that it was so they could attack the south and render Ahn's council of gods defenseless. But Navuh had his own agenda.

Areana sighed. "We should head back."

"I hope you do not regret what has happened here tonight."

She smiled. "The only thing I regret is having to stop. For the first time in seventy-one years, I feel alive. Thank you for that."

Her honesty was like a punch to his gut. But there was nothing he could do about it. She could never know about the schemes within schemes he was carefully orchestrating.

Taking her hand, he kissed the back of it. "No need to thank me. Not yet anyway." He winked.

Areana would think he had meant future sex, and he had, but she would have been much more grateful if she knew he was rescuing her from Mortdh. Except, if everything went right, she would never find out.

Bracing a hand against the flyer's side, he leaped out, and then reached with his arms and lifted her out of the vehicle.

As they walked back to camp, Areana glanced at him from beneath lowered lashes. "Will you come to visit me again like you did tonight?"

"I will do my best."

She chuckled. "Maybe you should wait until I reach the first coastal city and have a proper bath. I must stink. Are you sure you stopped for the reason you gave me?"

Again, he was struck by her honesty, and by how comfortable she seemed to be around him. Areana did not fear him. She thought of him as her ally, her co-conspirator.

It was a surprisingly pleasant feeling to have someone on his team, even if it was an illusion.

He lifted her hand for a kiss. "You smell sweet to me no matter how many days you were on the road without the benefit of a bath."

"It is very nice of you to lie to me like this. I will pretend I believe it."

He lied about so many things, but not about this. "It is not a lie."

They parted at the entrance to her tent. "Sleep well, Lady Areana, and have pleasant dreams." He winked at her.

"Oh, I will. Thank you. And the same to you, Lord Navuh. Thank you for the visit and all the good advice you have given me. I will discuss the new travel plans with the captain tomorrow."

He bowed, and then waited until she went inside, then turned and walked over to where her guards and the rest of the retinue huddled around a fire.

"Listen up, men," he said quietly but with the full power of compulsion. "Do not mention to anyone that I was here.

111

Do not even talk about it amongst yourselves. The only one you can mention me to is Lady Areana. Her safety depends on your discretion." He added the last sentence in case she could hear him. "Are my instructions clear?"

Eyes glazed and mouths slack, the men nodded.

He was about to walk away when he remembered the maid. "Where is the little girl? Lady Areana's maid?"

"She is sleeping in the wagon." An old human pointed at one of the five.

"Thank you."

Navuh strode to the one the man had indicated and lifted the flap. The girl was curled up on a bunch of pillows she had arranged in a row on the wagon's floor.

He climbed up and shook her shoulder. "Tula, wake up."

"Five more minutes," she mumbled.

Who did she think he was, her father? "Wake up, Tula."

As soon as she opened her eyes, the girl bolted upright. "Lord Navuh! What are you doing here?"

"Shh. I just wanted to tell you that you must keep my visit a secret."

Eyes glazing over, she nodded obediently.

"Tomorrow morning, you will wake up and not mention my visit to anyone other than Lady Areana."

She nodded again.

"Good girl." He ruffled her hair. "Go back to sleep."

Tula dropped as if he had pushed her down, and started snoring lightly.

The thing about compulsion was that it required accuracy. If he had not told her to wake up the next morning, the girl would have kept on sleeping until the compulsion was removed.

23

AREANA

*A*s the wagon swayed and bumped along the trail, Areana busied herself with a new embroidery project.

She was good at it, and her designs were lovely, but it was considered an unbecoming hobby for a goddess. Regrettably, none of the more acceptable pastimes, like composing poems, writing stories, and even painting pictures, could be done while riding in a wagon. Any of them would have been preferable to the mindless stitching which left her mind free to ponder her latest conundrum.

She wanted Navuh, but was about to mate his father.

Perhaps it would not have bothered other goddesses, but Areana was not the type to engage in clandestine affairs. Morally wrong in general, in her particular case having an affair was potentially deadly. Unlike other gods who upon discovering their partner's infidelity might have words with their unfaithful mate, Mortdh's retribution would be much worse.

With a sigh, she put the fabric down and leaned against a cushion.

Curiously, the wagon did not feel as stifling today as it had the day before. Maybe it was the promise of the coastal region's cooler climate that made it more tolerable. Or maybe everything seemed just a little brighter after last night.

Should she feel guilty?

After Ahnon's death, Areana had never expected to crave a man's touch again, let alone experience it and enjoy it. And yet, here she was, daydreaming about Navuh and impatiently waiting for their next meeting.

Then again, seventy-one years was long enough to mourn even a truelove mate. The pain of Ahnon's loss would never fade away completely, and she would never love another man like she had loved him, but she could see herself having a life with Navuh at her side.

It was strange how appealing she found him.

Firstly, he was an immortal and not a god, and secondly, he was the exact opposite of Ahnon in every possible way.

Except, she was much older now.

When Ahnon had started courting her, Areana was a young girl of seventeen who had seen the world with very different eyes than a two-hundred-and-thirty-seven-year-old woman. Her tastes were different now, as well as her cravings.

Or, perhaps, it had nothing to do with age and everything to do with Navuh. She would have found him just as appealing at seventeen as she did now. The main difference was that back then she would have felt too intimidated by Navuh to allow him to get close.

As the wagon stopped moving, Tula lifted the flap with a big grin on her face. "How would you like to wash in a cool spring, my lady?"

"There is a spring?"

"Yes. It is a little oasis in the middle of nowhere." She grimaced. "Unfortunately, every caravan driver and sheep-herder knows about it, so it is not like we will have privacy. But we can wash with our clothes on."

After days on the road, Areana had sand in unmention-able places that a wipe down with a wet washrag could not clean. She itched to submerge herself in water and wash everything from top to bottom. Doing so with clothes on just was not going to suffice.

Using Navuh's technique, she braced her hand on the wagon's side and leaped out instead of using the steps the driver put down for her. "I have a better idea. I can have the guards stand in a circle with their backs to us, blocking the view."

Tula clapped her hands. "That is an awesome idea! But are you sure they are not going to peek?"

"I am sure." She was not.

Sometimes, curiosity won over good manners, training, and even fear of retribution. But Areana was a goddess, and gods were not shy about their bodies. It did not mean that she would flounce around in the nude for everyone to see, but if a guard stole a peek, so be it.

Naturally, the captain was not too happy about her idea. "As you wish, my lady," he agreed with a barely suppressed grimace. "Let me assemble the men."

Standing in a circle, the water lapping at their middles, the guards were definitely uncomfortable in their wet clothes, holding their swords up so they would stay out of the water.

Her moans of pleasure and Tula's squeals of delight probably made it worse for them. The men had not availed themselves of female company for days. When they arrived at the first coastal city, she would tell the captain to give each man time off to find paid company.

With that in mind, Areana felt less guilty about taking her time to scrub her body and wash her hair and then do it all again while the poor soldiers stood guard.

Except, it would be weeks before they reached the first coastal city, which meant a long time for the men to wait for their reward. It also meant a long time until her next bath.

Unless there was another spring somewhere on the way.

"Are you done, my lady?" one of the soldiers asked.

"Almost." She turned to Tula. "Ready?"

"No." The girl sighed. "But I guess we have to. I still need to come back and do the laundry. It has to be done before sundown."

Areana reached for the clean dress that she had hung over a tree branch and pulled it over her head. Tula did the same with her tunic, and then collected their dirty things to add to her laundry pile.

There was no way to get out of the water without getting their fresh clothes wet, and by the time they reached the tent, Tula was shivering.

"Give me your dress, my lady. I will hang it out to dry."

"You should change out of your wet tunic first," Areana said as she removed the dress and put on a dry one.

"It is going to get wet anyway when I wash our things."

"That is true. But in the meantime, you should dry out and rest. You are shivering."

As Areana lay down on the cushions, she felt bad about Tula having to go back and do the laundry. She would have offered to help, but that would scandalize her guards even more than if she decided to parade naked through the campsite.

Goddesses were allowed to behave as they pleased, but not to do household chores.

"Is Lord Navuh going to come tonight too?" Tula asked as she added items to her growing laundry pile.

"Maybe. Why do you ask?"

The girl shrugged. "Maybe he saw another caravan while he flew over the sky. Perhaps he noticed Gulan."

Areana laughed. "I do not know what one can see from so high up, but not even Gulan is big enough to be seen from the skies."

"Oh." The girl's cheeks reddened.

"By the way, Tula. You should not mention Lord Navuh's visit to anyone. It is a most important secret."

"I know. He told me that I can only talk about it with you."

Areana frowned. "Were you out with the men when Lord Navuh left last night? I thought you were sleeping in the wagon."

"I was. He came inside and woke me up. Gave me a big scare."

"I can imagine. Especially in the dark."

Tula smirked. "He is very handsome. It is a shame he is the son of a crazy god."

"Shh, Tula, you should never talk like that." Areana sighed. "I really should start training you for court life. You need to learn proper manners and what is okay to say and what is not. Otherwise, you are going to get us both in trouble."

"I am sorry." The girl pouted.

24

ANNANI

"Good morning, my love." Khiann pulled Annani against his hard body and kissed her lips.

She opened one eye. "What time is it, and why are you waking me up so early?"

"It is two hours after sunrise, and I have to report to my father's office for work."

Wrapping her arms around him, Annani pulled Khiann on top of her. "No, you do not. Stay and make love to me."

"I can stay." He slid down her body and kissed the valley between her breasts. "And I can make love to you." He nuzzled her nipple. "But then I have to go to work."

"Why?"

"Because I do not want everyone to think I am a kept man, and that my only worth is satisfying their feisty princess."

Annani smirked. "But it is your most important job."

"Well, yes, it is. But other than being your sex toy, I also have obligations which I have neglected for long enough.

Threading her fingers through his hair, she gave a tug

and pulled his head up and away from her breast so he would look at her. "I do not want you to go."

"Can we talk about it after we make love?"

She let go of his hair. "We could do that."

Sliding further down her body he licked at her belly button.

It tickled, and she giggled. "Stop it! You are making me laugh."

"What is wrong with laughter?"

"Nothing. But it is not sexy."

"I beg to differ." He did it again and again until she was writhing under him, but for all the wrong reasons. "You are a monster, Khiann!"

"A tickle monster." He brushed his fingers against her waist, which he knew was incredibly sensitive to tickling.

"Okay, that is enough," she said in a stern tone.

"Maybe I should concentrate on another sensitive spot." He slid all the way down and flicked her slit with the tip of his tongue. "Is that better?"

"Oh, yes, much." She spread her legs wider. "Go to work, my sex toy."

That earned her a nip to the fleshy part of her thigh.

"Ouch."

"Behave," Khiann admonished before getting back to doing exactly what she had told him to.

He knew her body so well—how she liked to be touched and where, when it was okay to tease her, and when she was too impatient for games, and whether she was in the mood for sugar or spice.

Well, she was always in the mood for both, but there were degrees of sweetness and of spiciness. Luckily for her, Khiann was an excellent cook.

Figuratively speaking.

Her guy had never prepared a meal in his life, and

neither had she, but she was not a bad cook either, or rather a meal planner.

A morning romp, for example, required sweet and gentle, while nights were reserved for the more intense flavors.

As his fingers entered her sheath, and his lips closed around that most sensitive little nub, her climax rolled over her in a gentle wave instead of an explosion.

A moment later, Khiann replaced his finger with his manhood.

"I love you," she whispered as her arms tightened around him.

Instead of answering, he took her mouth in a hungry kiss, and his hips started moving faster.

She loved the feel of him.

Everything was so familiar, his weight, his size, the way he moved, his scent, even the grunts he emitted when nearing his peak.

But he was most magnificent when the glow of his eyes intensified a moment before he threw his head back and climaxed.

That was the beauty of sweet morning romps. The muted intensity allowed her to notice all those small things. More intense lovemaking was too distracting to pay attention to anything other than the coil tightening inside her.

Panting, he kissed her neck. "I love you, and I love our mornings together. I used to hate waking up early. Now, I cannot wait."

"And I cannot wait for nightfall."

For some reason, Khiann insisted on limiting his venom bites to once a day, or rather night. She would have to wait the entire day to get her fix.

Lifting on his elbows, he smiled at her with his fangs only partially elongated. "Join me in the washroom?"

"Sure."

In the bathtub, Annani sat between Khiann's spread thighs, with her back and head resting on his chest. "Can your father not find someone else to help him run his business?"

"He has trained me for years, and he trusts me. It will take him even longer to train someone who did not grow up in the business, and an employee is not the same as a son who has a vested interest in it."

Annani moved her hands in the water to make little waves. "What did your father do before you were born? And surely you were not much help as a little boy."

"He did everything himself."

"Exactly. He can go back to that until he trains a replacement for you."

"I would be letting him down."

She sighed. "I know you feel like that, but Navohn must realize that once you mated me things have changed. You no longer have only the obligation of a son to help his father. By joining with me, you joined the royal family and assumed new obligations."

"Your father does not need my help, nor did he ask for it."

"That is true. But just as I have to train at his side to learn how to be a ruler, so do you. Learning your father's craft has taken you years of apprenticing with him, and he has to worry only about selling, storing, and buying goods. Imagine how much more complicated Ahn's job is, and how many years it will take us to learn what he has to teach."

Khiann groaned. "No offense, love, but the prospect of apprenticing with your father does not appeal to me at all.

I hate politics, and the idea of dealing with a bunch of self-entitled, pompous gods day in and day out nauseates me."

Perhaps he should have thought of that before agreeing to mate her.

Then again, she had not made it clear that he would have to leave his merchant's way of life behind.

The truth was that there was no rush, and that Khiann could keep on doing what he loved for many years to come. By the time he would really need to start training with her father, it could very likely be that he would have gotten the traveling-merchant lifestyle out of his system.

Except, traveling outside the city walls was dangerous. Khiann was much safer in the palace, and that was why she wanted to keep him there. But then he would be miserable, which, to be frank, was an insult to her.

Was she not a good enough reason for him to want to hang around?

Did he not want to spend all of his waking hours with her the way she wanted to spend hers with him?

Did he not love her as much as she loved him?

"If you really loved me, you would stay by my side." It was an unfair thing to say, and she regretted the words as soon as they had left her mouth.

Except, Khiann took the bait and picked up the banter. "And if you really loved me, you would want me to be happy and do the things I love doing."

It was on.

"And if you really loved me, the thing you would love doing most is being with me…"

25

NAVUH

*A*s Mortdh's monthly procession moved slowly down the street, the humans waved and cheered. Sitting beside his father in the open carriage, Navuh observed the phenomenon and wondered whether they cheered out of genuine appreciation for their ruler or out of fear.

Grudgingly, Navuh had to concede that it was mostly the former and maybe just a little of the latter.

The one thing Mortdh knew how to do better than Ahn or any of the other gods was to connect with his human population.

He did not spend all his days sitting on his lavish throne and meeting only with the movers and shakers of the immortal and human societies. Once a month he rode through the streets, visited the most remote provinces, and talked with commoners.

The reason was not his father's love for the people, or any other noble sentiment like that.

Mortdh did not trust anybody, not his sons, not his advisors, and not anyone he had put in charge of anything.

He believed only in what he saw with his own eyes. By having his finger on the pulse of the people, he was not only well informed, but also almost impossible to manipulate.

"The people love you," Navuh said.

"As they should." Mortdh smiled and waved. "I am the one who is responsible for their prosperity. They know where their bread comes from."

"They respect you too."

"Naturally."

"Once you mate Ahn's daughter, they will hold you in even greater esteem."

The exchange was meant to manipulate Mortdh into doing what Navuh wanted him to do, and yet Areana's name could not pass his lips in the same sentence with Mortdh and joining.

It was a troubling development.

Lusting after Areana was acceptable, as was his desire to elevate his status by mating a goddess, but caring for her was dangerous. Early in his life, Navuh had learned not to let himself get close to anyone. Caring was a weakness that could be easily taken advantage of.

Especially by someone as ruthless as his father.

"Not the daughter that the son of a diseased goat has promised me. Areana is a nobody. If I mate her, I would lose respect, not gain it. I need to mate her sister."

"So maybe the best thing would be not to mate anyone. Annani is out of the picture, and the people respect and admire you despite her betrayal."

The word betrayal had the expected effect on Mortdh. His anger flared, the repugnant acrid scent increasing by the second.

Waving a hand, Mortdh cast a silencing shroud around

the carriage. "Once the usurper is dealt with, my honor will be restored," he hissed.

"No one would know to credit you with it."

"They will know."

"How are they going to? We are going to stage a bandit attack, and the people will believe that this is how he died. The usurper will not be the first god killed by bandits. It has happened before. Naturally, Ahn denied it, so officially no god was ever killed by humans, but the tales of it still circulate. Although, this gives me an idea. What if we circulate a rumor that you were the one who killed him? You do not even have to do it. A rumor should do."

As Navuh waited for Mortdh to take the bait, he forced his breathing to remain even.

For the next several moments, Mortdh was quiet, waving at the crowd with a forced smile plastered on his face. "I would relish killing him myself, but I do not want to end up in a tomb."

"You will not." Navuh could almost taste the invisible net closing around Mortdh. He had him exactly where he wanted him.

Turning as if to wave at the crowd on the other side of the carriage, Mortdh pinned Navuh with a hard stare. "I do not see how it can be done. I cannot make it known that the usurper died at my hand without the council coming after me."

Navuh leaned back in the seat and pretended nonchalance. "In order for the council to pass sentence, two reliable witnesses must see it done, report it, and provide testimony under oath. Without that definite proof, it does not matter what the rumors say, or even if you go around boasting about killing the god. The council cannot vote to convict you."

Mortdh narrowed his eyes. "Did you come up with this

plan right now, or have you given it a lot of thought beforehand?"

"My job is to offer you good advice and viable solutions to problems you have no time to deal with. I would have not been doing my duty if I did not explore all the possibilities. I had different ideas swirling around in my head, but the final details fell into place thanks to your input. However, it is up to you to do as you please with the information, Father."

"What do you think I should do?" Mortdh was still eyeing him suspiciously.

Navuh shrugged. "If it were me, I would do nothing. As I said, it is entirely up to you."

"You would not feel offended by the rejection and the breaking of a promise?"

"I probably would, and I certainly do feel offended on your behalf, but I am a patient man. I would wait for our army to be ready and then take the rule of the entire civilized world by force, or the threat of using it. Fear is a strong motivator."

The suspicion leaving Mortdh's eyes, he leaned back against the carriage's soft cushions. "I need to give it some thought. Maybe your way is more prudent."

Navuh nodded, his expression schooled into an indifferent mask. This was a huge success. He had managed to plant the idea in Mortdh's head while evading his father's suspicion.

There was little chance Mortdh would choose patience over the immediate gratification of vengeance.

It was not that Navuh was bloodthirsty, or that he cared whether Annani's mate lived or died. The unlucky god was going to die one way or another, either by an assassin's hand or Mortdh's.

Hopefully, it would be Mortdh's doing.

That way he would at least not die in vain. His murder would help put away for good a lunatic with too much power.

It would also serve Navuh's long-term agenda, but that was a side benefit. Navuh did not need the god's blood on his hands to achieve his ultimate goal. Once his army was strong enough, and his warriors learned to block the gods' mind-control powers, the gods would surrender without a fight.

He might even let them keep their temples and their worshipers, but he would strip them of all governing powers and tax their proceeds.

26

KHIANN

"Do you know what the summons is about?" Khiann asked his father as he met him outside Ahn's throne room.

"No, but I can guess. He probably wants me to release you from the obligation to work for me."

"Please do not. I am not ready to be cooped up in the palace and sit in on endless boring meetings."

Navohn sighed, his eyes filling with sorrow. "If he asks, I cannot say no."

More than Khiann's help in the business, Navohn just enjoyed having his son in the office, working side by side with him. Khiann liked it too. That was what he had trained for and had planned on doing since he was old enough to count coins. But then a little fiery princess burst into his life and turned all of his plans upside down.

Khiann loved her with everything he had, but he loved his father too and hated to disappoint him. Besides, he would much rather spend his workdays with his own father than with Annani's.

As the doors opened and a servant ushered them in,

Ahn stepped down from his dais.

"Welcome, my friend." He shook hands with Navohn. "And you, my son."

If calling Khiann his son was not shocking enough, Ahn also pulled him into a quick embrace and clapped him on the back.

The ruler had never acted in so fatherly a way toward him. Khiann did not need to be a mind reader to guess what was behind the sudden warmth, or rather who—a manipulative redhead who knew how to twist her father around her little finger.

"You are probably wondering why I invited you here today." Ahn led them to the two divans that had been brought into the throne room. "Please, make yourselves comfortable."

As soon as they sat down, a servant rushed to pour them drinks and load their plates with tasty treats.

Ahn rearranged his robes, spreading them evenly over his knees. "Now that the honeymoon period is over, and you are back at work, it is time to talk about your future, Khiann."

Yep. This had Annani written all over it. They were going to have words tonight. "What do you have in mind, my lord?" As if he did not know.

"I want you to start learning about politics. I think your time would be better spent by my side than in your father's office poring over ledgers and adding up numbers."

"That is not all I do."

Ahn waved a dismissive hand. "I know, I was exaggerating to make a point. But is it not what merchants do most of the time?"

"It is part of it, my lord," Navohn said. "But the really exciting part is traveling to distant lands and discovering new goods and bringing them home." He chuckled.

"Although I would be lying if I did not admit that counting profits is enjoyable too."

Taking a sip from his wine goblet, Ahn took a moment to come up with his next argument. "Politics is fascinating. I always feel like a juggler with fifty balls up in the air, spinning like a madman to keep any from falling. It can be quite exhilarating at times." He took another sip. "But I have to admit that sometimes it is frustrating as well. Now that both of you are part of the royal family, I can at least share some of those frustrations with you."

Khiann could not think of any frustration bigger than Mortdh's threat.

"I am honored that you think of me as family," Navohn said.

"I have always confided in you, my friend, but now I can do so with your son as well. It is a good thing to have two capable gods as my confidants."

"Indeed." Navohn inclined his head.

Khiann still did not know what the two were talking about. All he could think of was Ahn's demand that he quit working with his father.

"I am glad you think me worthy of your confidence, my lord, but I am sure you do not plan on stepping down anytime soon. I would like to stay and work for my father for a little longer. At least until we have trained another to replace me."

Navohn shook his head. "No one can replace you, Khiann. Someone can do your job, but no one can take the place of my beloved son."

Khiann was impressed.

His father was good. If after that sorrowful display Ahn still insisted on him leaving his father's side, the ruler would appear cruel.

"I know it is difficult, my friend. But we need to think

of Khiann's safety as well. Venturing outside the city walls is not wise at the moment. We do not know what Mortdh is planning, but I would be greatly surprised if he were not bent on revenge and arranging an assassination."

Khiann waved a hand. "I am well aware of the risks. But I am not some weakling god who cannot take control of several human and immortal brains at once. I can defend myself both with my mind and with my sword. I am also careful. I will take guards with me. What I am not willing to do is hide in the palace like a coward and live my life in fear."

Ahn smiled indulgently. "I had a feeling you would say that. And I do not doubt your ability to defend yourself, but perhaps you should weigh your need for freedom and adventure against the worry you are going to cause Annani." He lifted a brow. "Is it worth it?"

Apparently, it wasn't only his father who knew how to play the emotional blackmail game. Ahn seemed to be quite good at it himself. But Khiann was not going to let his mate or her father manipulate him.

As much as he loved Annani, he was still a man and not a rug under her feet. He had the right to make his own decisions.

"My mother worries every time my father leaves with a caravan, and yet she has never tried to stop him because she knows it is his passion."

Ahn chuckled. "You will do just fine in politics, Khiann. You have backbone." He lifted his goblet and tipped it in Khiann's direction. "I will grant you a few more years at your father's side. A good ruler should know all there is to know about commerce as well as about politics. But, eventually, I need you to come on board. There is much to be done."

Khiann let out a breath. "Thank you."

27

AREANA

"My lady." Tula slid down from the driver's seat, jumping the rest of the way and landing on the wagon's floor. "Do you want me to open the sides and let the sea breeze in?"

"That is a wonderful idea."

Areana had smelled the water hours ago, but until now the air had been arid and still. A sea breeze was most welcome.

Tula lifted the flaps and tied them back on one side of the wagon, then moved to do the same on the other. "Much better, right?"

"Indeed. Imagine how wonderful it will be when we actually reach the sea."

"I know. I cannot wait. But the driver says it will be at least two more hours before we get there. Probably three." Tula lifted the front flap separating the wagon from the driver's seat and climbed back up.

Sitting inside the wagon while it was moving made the girl nauseous. Or at least that was the excuse she had given

Areana for leaving her alone and spending her days upfront with the driver.

Areana did not mind. She was used to solitude.

Reaching into the basket, she picked up her embroidery project and resumed the stitching. The mindless work did not offer much distraction, though, and as was the case lately, her mind wandered to a certain dark and intense immortal.

Many days had passed since Navuh's visit.

After that night, Areana had listened for the sound of the flyer's engine every evening, and every night she had gone to sleep disappointed. Had she overestimated his interest in her?

It would be just like the rest of her rotten luck to finally fancy a male after decades of abstinence, but choose the worst candidate possible for her affections. Not only was he her intended's son, but apparently he was not all that interested in her, which, she had to admit, was for the best.

Navuh was smart and ambitious. He would not risk all that he had accomplished just because he lusted after a female. She should follow his example and do the same.

Instead, she was daydreaming about him like a silly young girl.

With a sigh, Areana lifted a spool of gold thread, cut a new length, and threaded it through the needle. The pattern she was stitching onto the ribbon was masculine, and the fabric was black—Navuh's favorite colors. Perhaps once she was done she would give it to him as a gift.

His seamstress could use it as a decoration for a new tunic.

Perhaps he was going to come tonight.

After all, she had told him to wait until she had a proper bath. Navuh either did not know about the spring she had washed in, or he did not think of it as proper bathing.

"My lady." Tula poked her head inside. "The cook is asking if we should stop for dinner or keep going until we reach an inn."

"Tell him to ask the captain. I am fine either way."

She had dried fruit and nuts to hold her over between meals, but the soldiers needed more substantial nourishment. She would not have them go hungry just because she was in a hurry to reach the coast.

A few moments later the wagon stopped. Evidently, the captain had decided in favor of an earlier dinner. At least there would be no need to erect tents, but the animals still had to be tended to.

Hopefully, the inn would have enough rooms for everyone in her small convoy. The men could sleep four to a room, and she and Tula could share one.

Except, what if Navuh came to visit her as he had implied he would?

If she had a room to herself, she could invite him to spend the night with her.

Was she that bold?

Or that desperate?

Once her dormant desires had been awakened, there was no going back to her old chaste existence.

How many nights had she lain awake and fantasized about what kind of a lover Navuh would be?

Nothing like Ahnon, that was for sure.

Navuh was a born leader, and as such he was probably more dominant than most. He would be intense and demanding.

How deliciously exciting.

She could imagine herself taking off the tie holding his hair back and threading her fingers through the midnight colored tresses. They would spill down his back, and when he lay on top of her, they would fall down like two curtains, framing his beautiful face and brushing over her heated skin.

"Ouch." A pinprick from her embroidery needle jarred her from her fantasies. Quickly, she lifted the injured finger to her mouth and licked off the tiny blood drop so it would not stain her project.

Fates, it had been so long since she had last felt the pleasure of a male's bite. Just the thought of it had her core moisten and then tighten painfully with need.

If the inn had enough rooms, she was definitely going to rent one for herself and another for Tula.

Hopefully, tonight she would not go to sleep disappointed again.

28

NAVUH

"*A*ny news from our spy network?" Mortdh asked.

All throughout their meeting, Navuh had been waiting for his father to ask that question. "Nothing overly interesting, other than the rumors about the usurper's plans to take a caravan west toward the Red Sea."

Mortdh lifted a brow. "I would say that is very interesting news. This is the chance we have been waiting for. He is finally leaving the safety of the city walls."

Regrettably, Mortdh had said we, and not I. Had he discarded the idea of murdering Khiann with his own hands?

"I have to substantiate the rumors first. We cannot plan an attack based on hearsay."

"And how do you propose to do that?"

"Other than the usurper and his father, the only one that has the exact travel plans is the father's assistant. Unfortunately, he is a strong immortal who is not easily influenced, and he cannot be bribed. I am afraid I will have to speak to him in person."

It was a lie, but it was the perfect excuse to borrow the

flyer and visit Areana. The little taste Navuh had gotten had only whetted his appetite for more. He had been aching for her ever since.

"That means at least two days' travel. To avoid notice, you'll have to arrive there near nightfall. You have to land far enough from the city so that no one spots the flyer, and you also need to find a good hiding place for it. Then, you have to wait for the next evening to come back."

"Is that a problem? I am not aware of you having air travel plans in the coming days."

Mortdh lifted his goblet and emptied its contents down his throat. "I do not. But I do not like it when you and my flyer are gone for more than a day."

Navuh wondered whether the reason was suspicion about what he was using the flyer for, or just Mortdh's usual possessiveness. He liked having his possessions and his underlings at his disposal at all times.

"I wish we had another flyer. That would solve a lot of problems for us."

"Right." Mortdh humphed. "And I wish we had more than two tablets with functioning communication capabilities. What is the use of having one when the only other belongs to Ahn? If I could have given one to our master spy in Ahn's capital, we could have had immediate access to all the latest news instead of relying on a primitive relay system. Our technology is crumbling, and we do not have replacement parts to fix what is broken, and no way of manufacturing them. In time, nothing is going to be left of it, and we are going to have to live as primitively as the humans."

Mortdh did not talk much about their people's history. One of the few things he had shared with Navuh was that it had been thousands of years since the boat of a million years had visited earth, bringing new supplies and loading up with earth's precious metals.

"I wonder why they abandoned you here."

Mortdh lifted his goblet for Navuh to refill. "There could be several reasons. They might have found a better source that is closer to the home world. Their scientists might have invented a new process to convert easily obtained materials into whatever else they needed. Or they might have blown themselves to pieces. The communicator stopped working thousands of years ago."

He took a long sip from the wine Navuh had poured. "Bottom line, we are on our own, and no one is watching. That is why I decided to take control away from Ahn. It is not as if my grandfather is going to pay us a surprise visit and smite me for disobeying him and dethroning his chosen son."

Navuh stifled a smile. Evidently, every cat was a mouse to a larger cat, and when that cat was not watching, the mice were having a party.

The problem was that his cat was watchful and suspicious. On the other hand, Navuh was more of a rat than a mouse. "If it is agreeable to you, Father, I will leave later this evening and return tomorrow night."

Mortdh waved a hand. "Do I have a choice? If I want to end the life of that miserable son of a diseased goat, I need to have reliable information about his travel plans."

29

AREANA

*A*s Areana waded into the sea, Tula stayed on the shore and eyed the water suspiciously. "I do not know how to swim, my lady."

"I can teach you."

The girl shook her head. "It is too dark, and no one is here."

"It is not too dark for us. And it is good that we have the beach to ourselves. Here," Areana said as she intensified her glow. "Is that better?"

It was only late evening, and the sky was not entirely dark. There was plenty of light for an immortal to see by.

Reluctantly, Tula took a step in. "It is cold."

"Come on, Tula, do not be such a scared rabbit. Where is that feisty attitude of yours?"

Tightening her lips, Tula waded to where Areana was standing waist-deep in the water. "I do not want to go any deeper."

"That is fine. We can swim parallel to the shore so you can touch the bottom with your feet anytime you need to. Now watch what I do and follow my moves."

It felt amazing to swim in the cool water, and after several strokes Areana flipped to her back and floated, looking up at the darkening sky. "I could stay like this for hours."

Next to her, Tula did the same, but instead of floating, she flailed and swallowed seawater. "Yuk. It is disgusting." She spat, making a face.

Areana laughed. "You need to hold your body straight, balance, and move your arms like this."

Tula's next attempt was more successful, and she floated next to Areana. Only four soldiers had accompanied them to the beach, while the rest took care of finding a stable for the animals and a secure place to park the wagons so nothing would get stolen.

"It is fun," Tula admitted.

"How come you never learned how to swim? We live right next to the coast."

Well, she no longer did, but Tula might go back once she'd convinced Gulan to come home with her.

"I never wanted to. My mother told me that there were predatory fish in the water and that it was dangerous, especially for a human. I only turned immortal recently."

Areana had forgotten about that. The girl was new to her powers.

"What can you do now that you could not do before?"

Making large circles with her arms, Tula was working harder on staying afloat than was needed. "I am stronger and can lift heavier things. I can run faster, and I can hear and see better. I can also smell better."

"Can you thrall?"

"A little."

"That is good. Thralling is very useful in case humans attack you. The trick is to keep cool. If you panic, you will not be able to concentrate enough for thralling."

"I know. I have been practicing with Gulan. But then she just left me and ran away. How could she do this to me?" Tula's voice quivered.

"Oh, my dear girl." Areana reached and took her hand. "Gulan did not run away from you. She ran away from her pain. I could have told her that it would not work because she would be taking the pain with her. But she did not ask my advice."

"It is not like the love of her life died. She got her feelings hurt by that stupid Esag. Big deal. I thought she was stronger than that."

For the first time in forever, the mention of Ahnon's loss did not bring tears to Areana's eyes, nor did a choking lump lodge in her throat. Was she finally over it?

The pain was still there, but it felt muted somehow, tolerable.

Dropping her legs down, Areana stood in the water. "In her mind, Gulan has lost the love of her life. Once enough time passes, she might think differently, especially when she finds a new love interest, but right now she is grieving the loss of her dream, of what could have been."

Tula started wading out of the water. "I think that what she did was selfish, and once I see her, I am going to tell her that."

Following behind, Areana chuckled. "That is not the best strategy for convincing her to come home with you."

"So what? I am her sister, and I am allowed to tell her what I think about her stupid escape. She is a coward."

Interesting observation. Did it apply to Areana as well? Had she grieved for so long and avoided male attention because she was scared of getting hurt again?

Subconsciously, she must have feared to lose another person she loved, and therefore refrained from forming new relationships.

Increasing her pace, Tula pushed through the water as if those predatory fish her mother had warned her against were chasing her. "If it were me, I would have punched Esag in his stupid smiling face and told him never to even look my way. Then I would have flirted with every guy he knew to get him jealous."

"Why? To make him realize his loss? Would you have taken him back?"

The girl stopped and turned around. "No way! I would do it for vengeance."

NAVUH

*B*y Navuh's calculations, Areana should have reached the first coastal town on the map he had shown her.

Just to be sure, though, he scanned the caravan routes leading west toward the coast as he flew over them. This late in the evening, the roads were deserted, but he had not spotted any encampments either.

Landing an hour or so walking distance from the city, he parked the flyer behind an outcropping of boulders and pulled out the commoner garb he had hidden under its seat.

Between the simple clothes and the long headdress that obscured most of his face, no one was going to recognize him or pay him any attention.

There were only two inns in the small town, and Navuh gambled that Areana would be in the larger and pricier one.

It took little effort to thrall the human innkeeper into telling him about the highborn lady who had arrived earlier with her armed escort and had rented all of the rooms on the second floor.

Areana had been smart to hide her godly identity. The innkeeper had not even known that the lady staying at his inn was not human.

Finding her room was easy. The two guards standing to attention outside her door gave it away.

"Lady Areana is expecting me." He infused his voice with compulsion. "Knock on her door and tell her she has a visitor."

The guard on the left did as he asked, while the one on the right stared at him with drool dripping from one side of his mouth.

Evidently, he had used too much force. Some immortals were more susceptible than others, and some were resistant. Without knowing the person, it was hard to tell how much was needed.

"You may go in," the first guard said.

The other one had wiped off the drool and was shaking his head.

"Thank you. Stay on guard but forget I am in there. Your lady is safe with me."

The guard nodded and opened the door for him.

"I thought it might be you," Areana said as he entered. "How come my guards did not recognize you?"

Navuh closed the door behind him and locked it. "My disguise fooled them."

She eyed him suspiciously. "And they let you in even though they did not know who you were?"

"You told them to let me in. Soldiers do not question orders from their superiors."

"Maybe in your experience, but not in mine."

Navuh took the headdress off and tossed it aside. Areana was asking all the wrong questions.

"Can you cast a silencing shroud?"

"Yes, but not a very good one." Areana waved a hand.

She was right. It was not very good, but it would do.

"You did not ask me why I am here." He took a step toward her.

She did not back away, but her pulse sped up, and she swallowed nervously. "I know why you are here."

He took another step until they were standing chest to chest. "I will ask only once. Do you want me to be here?"

Lifting her eyes to his, she nodded. "I do." Her pulse was now racing faster than a rabbit's.

He would give her one more chance to change her mind. Hooking a finger under her chin, he planted a soft kiss on her lips. "If you tell me to leave, I will. There is no pressure, Areana. I want you, but I will not settle for anything less than everything you have to give."

Enough females gave themselves to Navuh because they thought it was expected of them, or because they sought an elevated status and monetary rewards. He did not want Areana like that.

If she gave herself to him, it would be because she craved him as much as he craved her. "Take a moment to think it through and decide if you are ready for this. If you are not, I will understand, and I will not hold it against you. You have my word."

He even meant it.

"I do not need a moment." Areana wrapped her arms around his neck and loosened the tie holding his hair back. "This is all I could think of doing since you left me and promised to come back." She threaded her fingers through his long, straight hair and fanned it out.

Attempting to put her at ease, he arched a brow and smiled. "This was the only thing? My hair?"

"Among other things." She lowered her eyes to his chest

and put her hands on his pectorals. "I also wanted to do this."

"I have had a few things of my own in mind." He put his hands on her slim waist, lifted her up, carried her to the bed, and laid her down. "Take off your dress for me, Areana, and let me see you."

He took a step back and waited.

AREANA

*I*t had been so long since Areana had stripped for a male.

She wanted to do it seductively, to draw it out and heighten Navuh's desire. Instead, she felt clumsy and ungraceful as she lifted her hips and pulled her dress up, baring the lower part of her body first, when the proper way to strip was to start with the top.

Except, the heat in Navuh's gaze assured her that it did not matter to him.

"Let me help you with that," he said in a voice so low that it sounded more like a growl. A hiss escaped his lips as he tugged her dress over her head. "I have imagined you like this for years, but your beauty exceeds all of my expectations."

Areana was taken aback. "You have dreamt about me for years?"

"I have ached for you since I was a boy. But you were always beyond my reach. All I could do was dream."

Leaning, he cupped the back of her neck and pressed a

soft kiss on her mouth. "I have especially dreamed of those lips." He smirked. "But not only about kissing."

Areana felt her cheeks warm. She was not a novice and knew what he was hinting at, but she had never done it. Ahnon had not expressed a desire to be pleasured that way, and although she would have gladly complied if he had asked, she had never thought of the act as something that could be pleasing to a female. Therefore, she had not volunteered.

"What is the matter, beautiful?" He cupped her heated cheek. "Are you suddenly shy?"

Fates, he had the most seductive voice, and the confident, taunting tone was enough to make her swoon. But she still had a few tricks of her own. Some things a woman never forgot how to do.

Lying back, she lifted her arms over her head and stretched, putting her long body on display for him. She was a bit too lean and could have used a little more feminine curves, but she knew that her body was pleasing to the eye nonetheless. Even though her breasts were small and her hips narrow, everything was perfectly proportionate.

"No, I am not shy. How about you?" She arched a brow.

Navuh was still dressed, and the commoner's disguise he was wearing was not flattering. Unlike his own refined clothes, which were all made from fine black cloth and gold accents, the rough brown fabric and the billowing width did not accentuate his beautiful physique.

"I am not shy either." He pulled the tunic over his head, revealing smooth muscles that tapered into a narrow waist.

Just like his face, his body was all perfectly chiseled angles and hardness. There was nothing soft about Navuh, not on the outside and not on the inside.

Untying the braid holding up his pants, he let both fall to the floor and stepped out of them, proudly nude.

Areana sucked in a breath.

Navuh was a sight to behold—power and beauty combined to create a male who was more of a god than any immortal had the right to be.

"You are perfect," she whispered.

He put one knee on the bed. "I am glad you think so."

Leaning over her, he blanketed her with his big body, but instead of letting her bear his weight, his chest hovered a hand span away from hers, depriving her of the skin to skin contact she craved.

"Look at this." Pushing back to straddle her hips, he put both hands on her belly. "My dark to your pearly luminescence. It is poetic."

He seemed awed by her, which pleased her greatly, but all Areana could think about were those hands of his touching her all over.

He did, but not in the way she wanted.

Avoiding her aching breasts, his fingers feathered over her skin, drawing lines of fires everywhere they touched.

In no time, she was panting for more, but Navuh seemed in no hurry. If not for his harsh breathing, which was just as ragged and uneven as hers, she would have thought him unaffected.

His eyes were glazed with desire, but his facial expression revealed next to nothing.

Such tremendous self-control was both admirable and intimidating.

Compared to him, she had none. Gripped by the power of her lust, she could hide nothing from those penetrating eyes, baring to him much more than her body.

What was happening to her?

Her seven-decade-long abstinence had been more of a

state of mind than an exercise in restraint. With no desire, there had been no need to fight it. But with that state of mind irrevocably changed, she was shivering all over, the lightest of touches setting her on fire.

Except, they did not stay light for long.

As Navuh slid his palms down her shoulders and around her breasts, Areana barely dared to breathe. Mesmerized, she gazed upon his beautiful face, the dark shadows his long hair was casting on the hollows of his cheeks, and the intense fire burning in his dark eyes that made him look more demonic than godly.

He was terrifying, and yet irresistible.

After what seemed like a long moment suspended in time, the feel of his large hands on her breasts was so sudden and unexpected that Areana arched up sharply.

It was as if she had been zapped by lightning.

"Please," she groaned, not knowing what she was asking for.

More? Less?

As an answer to her plea, his fingers rimmed her pebbled nubs and then pinched lightly.

The tiny ache ratcheting up her desire, she let out a throaty moan.

Satisfied with her response, Navuh smirked and then dipped his head, taking one bud into his mouth and soothing the tiny ache with gentle flicks of his tongue. He then moved to the other.

Fates, the man knew what he was doing.

Overwhelmed by the sensations bombarding her, Areana closed her eyes, only to force them open a split moment later. She did not want to miss anything. Watching Navuh masterfully play her body was just as exhilarating as experiencing his touch.

Bringing her arms around him, she smoothed her palms over his hard muscles.

A growl started deep in his chest, a split second warning before his blunt front teeth closed around her turgid nub. It did not hurt. But then his fully extended fangs scraped the soft flesh of her breast, piercing her skin. It should have been painful, but in her highly aroused state, the little pinpricks only added fuel to her excitement.

He licked the tiny wounds and then hissed, "Keep your arms over your head."

"Why? I like touching you."

"Do not ask why. Just do it."

She had expected him to be commanding, it was part of his appeal, but not this autocratic tone.

It cooled some of her fervor. "I need to know why."

He lifted his head, his stern expression sending shivers down her spine.

"I told you that I would not settle for anything less than everything you have to give, and that includes your obedience."

Areana swallowed. She had accepted Navuh's terms without thinking, or rather thinking in terms she was familiar with. Ahnon had never demanded her obedience, and if he had, she would have denied him.

Except, Navuh was not Ahnon, and obeying him sexually excited her for some reason.

She nodded. "Only in this."

"That is all I am asking for."

NAVUH

or now.

Eventually, he would have her willing obedience in everything.

Control was important to Navuh, and his careful planning demanded that everyone around him did exactly as they were told.

Always, and without exception.

Optimally, people would cede control to him because it was in their best interest to do so, and not because of fear of retribution. But if needed, he had no problem using intimidation to get what he wanted.

Complying, Areana lifted her arms over her head. "At your command, my lord."

A full-blooded goddess referring to him as her lord was most satisfying. Especially when that goddess was Areana. She had no idea how much he loved those words coming out of her mouth.

They evoked images of those lush lips of hers wrapped around his shaft, his hand fisting her hair and holding her in place for his thrusts.

As much as that would have pleased him, though, it was not going to happen tonight. From her earlier reaction, it was obvious that Areana had never done that for her mate, which he found most curious.

Truelove mates were supposed to crave pleasuring their partners in every possible way. Even Navuh, who had not felt love for any of his concubines, had striven to provide them with as many orgasms as they could take. It was a matter of pride. And since he had not met a male who did not enjoy that particular form of pleasuring, he had to assume that Areana had denied her mate, which was inconceivable if they had been each other's trueloves.

Was it possible that they were not?

How did one determine that? And what was the difference between regular love and truelove?

Did it mean that Areana could belong to him body and soul?

This was more than he had ever hoped for, but he would have to ponder those questions later. Right now, he had the beautiful goddess under him, awaiting his skillful touch, and he needed to teach her that her obedience would be rewarded with more pleasure than she thought possible.

Sliding his hands down her body, he slowly skimmed her narrow hips, and as he smoothed his palms up her inner thighs, Areana parted her legs in invitation. Cupping her heated center, he hissed as her welcoming wetness sent a bolt of desire into his shaft.

Here she was, sprawled before him, giving herself to him so beautifully, so completely. It was better than he had ever imagined.

"Are you aching for me, Areana?" He slipped a finger into her wet sheath.

She gasped, and then looked at him with hooded eyes, their inner light painting circles on his chest. "Yes."

"You are so lovely to me." He withdrew his finger and came back with two.

On a moan, she closed her eyes, but then immediately blinked them open again. "You are lovely to me as well."

Navuh was a prideful male, but Areana's appreciative gaze made him even prouder. Her eyes did not leave him for longer than it took her to blink.

Pulling his fingers out, he trailed them up her wet folds to the center of her desire and circled the little nub without touching it directly.

That, he was going to do with his tongue.

"Oh." Areana lifted up, seeking more friction.

Slowly, he slid down her body while holding her gaze, then lowered his head and licked her slit, parting the folds.

"Beautiful," he murmured against her soft petals.

Her legs quivering, Areana panted, a small whimper escaping her mouth.

Was she afraid?

Was she unaccustomed to this form of pleasure as well?

Should he ask?

Better not. It would only embarrass her. Instead, he pushed his hands under her bottom and pressed a gentle kiss to her lower lips.

"Lovely," he reassured her.

Areana relaxed, the tight muscles of her small bottom loosening in his grasp. She was so delicately built and seemingly fragile that he had to remind himself that she was almost indestructible, and that he did not need to be so careful with her.

Except, unlike all the other gods and goddesses, this one was worthy of his worship, and Navuh was going to do so with his hands and his mouth and with every other part of his body.

None was more deserving than his Areana.

As another soft kiss and then another made her sigh contentedly, he upped the ante and licked inside her.

She tensed again, but the outpour of nectar on his tongue hinted that it was because the coil inside her was tightening and not because she was apprehensive.

When he moved his attention to the little nub at the apex of her womanhood, Areana cried out. And as he flicked it again with his tongue, and then again, going harder and faster, her cries got louder and louder.

Areana was nearing her climax, but he did not want her to orgasm yet. Pulling his mouth away, he slid up her body.

"Why did you stop?"

He kissed her throat, and then licked it, letting his fangs scrape against her nearly translucent skin. "I want to be inside you when you reach your peak."

33

AREANA

*T*ears misted Areana's eyes. She had been so close. Why had he stopped?

She had not expected to enjoy this form of carnal pleasure, had never understood its appeal, but Navuh had changed her mind about it. At first, she had thought to protest, but then she had remembered her promise of obedience and relented.

Maybe that was what had made the difference?

Or had it been Navuh's obvious delight in pleasuring her with his mouth?

"Why did you stop?"

He kissed her throat and then licked it. "I want to be inside you when you reach your peak."

The weight of his body on top of her felt delicious, as did the feel of his manhood probing her entrance. When his fangs scraped along the column of her neck, the coil inside her tightened again.

Was he going to bite her?

Fates, how she missed that. Nothing compared to the

venom-induced bliss. As she remembered it, the bite had often been the best part of the lovemaking.

Kissing up her throat, he reached her lips and thrust his tongue inside her mouth, silencing her cry as he speared into her womanhood.

After decades of abstinence, Areana had expected it to hurt, and at first, it did a little, but it did not detract from the rightness of the moment. It was as if their bodies were made for each other, the fit snug but perfect.

The feeling of utter satisfaction was entirely unexpected.

Seating himself all the way inside her, Navuh wrapped his strong arms around her and held her close. "I have never felt more at home than I do now."

If she were not echoing the same feeling, Areana would have thought he was just feeding her a nice line.

With his long black hair spilling down like two silk curtains around them, she felt cocooned with him, sheltered from the world, and she never wanted to leave.

"Make love to me, Navuh," Areana whispered into the crook of his neck.

Lifting up on his arms, he held her gaze as he pulled back, then speared inside her again. Going harder and faster, he swiveled his hips, hitting the apex of her womanhood with every thrust.

A few more of those and she was going to climax so hard that the earth was going to shake from the force of the explosion.

"You belong to me, Areana," Navuh hissed into her ear.

She was too far gone to argue.

Right now, she was his, and now it was all that mattered. Reality had no bearing on this stolen magical moment between them.

As their bodies moved together with increasing

urgency, the carnal dance bringing them closer and closer to the jagged edge, Navuh's grunts got harsher and his thrusts faster and harder.

Instinct taking over, Areana turned her head and offered him her neck. "Bite me," she breathed.

Wresting restraint from Fates knew where, Navuh licked the spot before emitting a loud hiss and sinking his fangs into her skin.

The venom bite should have been momentarily painful, but Navuh's preparation minimized the sting, or perhaps it was the distracting effect of the orgasm barreling through her.

Even before the venom had a chance to hit her system, rapture exploded through her, triggering Navuh's completion. Throwing his head back, he growled her name as his shaft swelled, and with one last powerful thrust, he erupted inside her, filling her with his essence.

Waves upon waves of pleasure exploded outward like the earth tremors from an epicenter, the sensations so intense that Areana almost regretted when the venom-induced bliss washed over her, replacing that intensity with mind-numbing euphoria.

Long moments later, she came down from soaring up in the clouds, glad to feel Navuh's weight. He had not moved while she was gone, his big body still shuddering as he waited for her to come back to him.

Wrapping her arms around him, she kissed the side of his moist neck. "That was intense."

What Areana had really wanted to say was that it had been the best sex of her life, but that would have been disrespectful to Ahnon's memory.

As amazing as the sex with Navuh had been, it was all about physical pleasure.

She did not love him, and he did not love her.

What she and Ahnon had shared was irreplaceable. They had loved each other since they were kids, and when they had mated, there had been lots of passion.

So what if their lovemaking had not been as explosive?

Mates grew accustomed to each other. Once the craziness of the initial attraction waned, couples settled into a comfortable routine. In time, the intensity was replaced with familiarity.

Except, a small voice inside her head whispered that with Navuh things would never settle into easy companionship. He was not the type of male who made anyone feel comfortable in his presence. As a lover, he was exciting, even exhilarating, but as a life partner, he was probably too overbearing.

Still, she would have chosen Navuh a thousand times over his father.

As far as she knew, Mortdh had no redeeming qualities. In fact, he disgusted her. Before agreeing to the mating, she had only seen him from afar. Like all gods, he was exceedingly good-looking—perhaps even more than most. Nevertheless, she had been indifferent to him as a male.

But then, she had felt that way about males in general.

It had taken standing close enough to Mortdh for Areana to smell the repugnant scents of his arrogance and disdain. But the final catalyst to transform her indifference into repulsion had been his disrespectful *used goods* comment.

Uncharacteristically of her mellow and gentle nature, she found herself wishing for Mortdh's death. With him gone, everyone's troubles would be over.

She could make a life with Navuh, Annani and Khiann could live in mated bliss without fearing the mad god, and Ahn could sleep peacefully knowing that no one was about to challenge his rule.

Tightening her arms around Navuh, Areana wished she was more like her half-sister—brave and determined. Annani would have found a way to kill the god and even get away with it.

But Areana was not Annani. She was a timid goddess with very limited powers. Regrettably, Mortdh had nothing to fear from her.

34

ANNANI

"I do not want you to go." Annani pouted.

It was futile. She had tried every argument she could think of. She had cried and begged. But nothing had been able to change Khiann's mind.

He had gotten it into his thick head that he would be letting his father down if he did not stick to the commitment he had made to lighten his burden. Khiann planned on taking over every other caravan so his father could spend more time at home with his mother.

Or at least that was the reason he was sticking to.

Annani suspected that it was a matter of pride. Khiann did not want people to think of him as the princess's mate. He wanted to be his own man. And the way he sought to do that was to keep doing what he had been training for since boyhood.

Khiann pulled her into his arms. "We have talked about it, love. You can come to visit me every night, and it will be as if I never left. Just make sure to bring the Odus with you when you fly over."

"I can bring soldiers."

"I trust the Odus more."

"Why? They are trained as servants."

"This is what they do, not what they are capable of. You know that they served a different purpose before. Besides, they are indestructible. If something happens to your flyer, like a mechanical malfunction, they can encircle you with their bodies and save you from a lot of pain or even death. We do not know if we can survive a fall from the sky. Our healing abilities have limits."

She put her hands on her hips. "We also do not know what the Odus can do and how indestructible they really are."

Leaning down, Khiann tapped her nose with his finger. "Yes, we do. You were with me when Ekin explained their programming. Their primary objective is to keep you safe."

"I see that nothing I can say is going to change your mind. You are so stubborn."

"Look who is talking."

That was true. When Annani set her mind on something, there was little anyone could do or say to deter her from achieving it.

Except for her stubborn mate who, apparently, was immune to her manipulations.

She poked his chest with her finger. "I am going to come to you every night."

"I am counting on it."

"And I am going to bring you dinner."

"You mean, bring us dinner. We will dine together."

"Yes, of course, that was what I meant. Are you taking a big tent with you? I want to sleep comfortably at night."

Khiann arched a brow. "Who is going to be sleeping? I plan on making love to you all night long."

"And when are you going to sleep?"

"I will make myself a bed in one of the caravans and sleep on the way."

"Hmm, that is actually not a bad idea. I can switch to sleeping during the day as well." She smirked. "It will provide me with the perfect excuse to wiggle out of throne room attendance."

Leaning, so he was practically bent in half, Khiann took her lips in a passionate kiss. "We will be spending as much time together on the road as we do now. It is going to be fun."

Annani grimaced. "There are no bathing facilities on the road. I will come home in the morning and wash the sand off. But what about you? After a few days on the road, you are going to stink."

"I will take a large supply of aromatic lotions, and I will clean myself as thoroughly as I can with washrags."

Khiann was proving to be even worse than her. "You have an answer for everything, do you not?"

"Not for everything, but for most of them. Stop fretting. I will start thinking that I have joined with a spoiled princess."

She slapped him playfully. "Of course, you did. Not only that, but you also promised to spoil me even more."

"I do not remember such a pledge."

"You did, and I can quote it word for word." Annani cleared her throat and then continued in a deepened voice. "I, Khiann, son of Yaeni and Navohn, promise to spend the rest of my life making you happy and thanking the Fates and your parents for the precious gift of you."

"I promised to make you happy, not to spoil you."

Stifling a smile, Annani shrugged. "It is the same thing. To me, it sounds like you are trying to wiggle out of your promise."

35

NAVUH

"*I* have a private matter I need to discuss with you, Father." Navuh hinted that the rest of their meeting should take place without witnesses.

With a wave of his hand, Mortdh dismissed his secretary and two servants. As soon as the doors closed behind them, he cast a silencing shroud around the chamber.

"Do you have information about the usurper's travel plans?"

"I do." Navuh's spies in Ahn's palace had provided all the necessary information.

Despite the story he had told Mortdh about having to verify the merchant's exact travel timeline, there was no need. Evidently, the princess had been quite vocal about her opposition to her mate's travel plans, and their arguments had been overheard.

"He leaves in eight days, heading west. But there is a small complication. Apparently, the princess plans on flying over and visiting him every night, accompanied by her Odus."

The biomechanical servants were a real threat to a god,

even the most powerful one. No wonder they had been destroyed, and further creation of them had been banned.

Annani's seven were probably the only ones still in existence.

They could not be thralled, they could not be destroyed, and information they reported would be beyond contestation. Besides, Annani might command them to defend Khiann.

Mortdh got up and started pacing. "Then we have to strike during the day before she gets there. Does she plan on visiting him while he is on the road, or only when he stops for the night?"

"According to our spies in the palace, she plans on visiting him at night in his tent."

Mortdh still had not indicated whether he was going to do it himself or send assassins.

"How many guards is he taking with him?"

"Ten immortal warriors from Ahn's palace guard."

A wicked smile twisted Mortdh's mouth. "Ahn is leaving the palace exposed with only skeleton defenses. Between the twelve accompanying Areana and the ten going with the usurper, how many warriors could be left to guard the palace?"

"Enough."

Ahn's garrison was comprised of over two hundred well-trained immortal warriors. Other than that, every immortal male of age in his territory was required to attend basic training and could be drafted in time of need. That expanded the size of his possible army from a couple of hundred into several thousand.

Mortdh waved a hand. "It was just a thought. Unfortunately, we cannot launch an armed assault until our soldiers learn to shield their minds. It is going frustratingly slowly."

"It is a process of elimination. Only about five out of twenty can be taught to effectively shield against thralling. When we have several hundreds of those, we will be ready."

Mortdh nodded. "That is why the breeding program is so important. We need to increase the rate of production."

"I have thought of a way to do it, provided it meets with your approval." Navuh was veering from the subject he wanted to focus on, but it was a good strategic move. He should not appear too eager, lest his father suspect that he had an interest in Khiann's assassination.

"Do tell."

"A repurposing of your fertility temples."

Mortdh frowned. "I happen to like the way they are run. I wrote the protocol."

When his father had eliminated civil rights for females, he had also done away with the fertility goddess worship, which had been hugely popular. Now the temples were dedicated to him, and he took much pleasure in personally inducting the virgin priestesses.

"I am not talking about changing the way new priestesses are inducted, only about who we recruit to serve in the temples and how long we keep them."

That seemed to appease Mortdh. "Continue."

"In addition to the humans, we collect young Dormant females who have not transitioned yet and we don't allow them to. In the temple, they will serve human males only, and since they will remain human themselves, their conception rate will be as high as that of regular humans. We are talking ten or more children per female. The male children will get inducted into immortality and join our army, while the female children will join their mothers in the temple and produce more children. In one century, we can have a sizable army that would have otherwise taken us a thousand years to produce."

Mortdh grinned, looking the happiest Navuh had seen him in a while. "I knew I made the right choice when I appointed you as my second-in-command. This is a brilliant idea. The only problem I can see is the unrest it will cause. People are going to be unhappy about their daughters not being allowed to transition and serving humans. Also, if we restrict the temple services to human males only, we will have to find a different solution for our immortal warriors. In order to keep the Dormants from transitioning, we cannot allow immortal males anywhere near them."

"Those are good points. I have not worked out all the details yet, but we can have two different kinds of temples. One will be staffed with Dormant females and serve humans, while the other will be staffed with human females and serve immortal males."

"I like it. What about the unrest?"

"I will have to ponder it some more."

"You do that. But first, let us finalize the details of getting rid of that parasite who stole my intended. To implement your plan without having a rebellion on our hands, people need to fear me. I need to avenge my honor and show that no one crosses me and lives, not even a god."

Navuh stifled a relieved breath. "Do we use assassins and just spread the rumor that the usurper died by your hand, or are you planning on doing it yourself?"

"Either could work, but I prefer doing it myself, and not only because I will derive immense satisfaction from beheading that parasite. The last thing I want is for another rumor to start circulating about me being a fraud and taking credit for something I have not done. Killing him myself is the only way I can restore my honor and plant fear in the hearts of my enemies. I just need a fail-proof plan for avoiding the fucking god council's judgment. I assume you have one?"

He did, but it had little to do with providing his father with a good alibi and everything to do with keeping Mortdh away from the palace and not asking about Areana.

"I do. I suggest we wait at least two weeks, attacking when the caravan is halfway to its destination and in the middle of nowhere. In the meantime, you should go on one of your long tours with as much fanfare as possible."

Mortdh loved touring his territory, and especially his visits to the fertility temples where new virgin priestesses were waiting for inductions.

His father smoothed his hand over his beard. "Easy to arrange."

"In about two weeks, I will arrive with the flyer and the three elite warriors that I will personally train for the mission. I will hide it out of sight, and when you depart with it the next day, I will stay in your tent and pretend to be you. Naturally, you will have to dismiss your servants and your assistants and demand that they do not bother you."

Mortdh smoothed his hand over his beard. "I will do that, and I will also thrall my guards to forget that they saw me leave and to keep everyone out. When I return, I will thrall them again for good measure. Just stay inside the tent and out of sight."

Navuh bowed his head. "As you wish, Father."

36

NAVUH

*A*s the sun began its descent, Navuh lifted his hand, calling a halt to the afternoon training session he had come to observe.

"Good job, men."

The young soldiers bowed, and then headed to their barracks.

"The youngsters are starting to look like real warriors." He clapped their captain on his back.

"Thank you, my lord." The man bowed.

Thankfully, that had been the last task on Navuh's list for the day, and he could finally retire to his private quarters and get some rest.

His fatigue was not physical. It was mental.

Several days had passed since he had last seen Areana, and he had been aching for her ever since. After having a taste of a goddess, none of his immortal concubines would do.

The thought of slaking his needs with an inferior female was as enticing as drinking muddy water after having tasted the nectar of the gods.

He would rather stay thirsty.

For the first time since his boyhood, his nightly mistress had been his own hand—his inspiration a pale and delicate goddess who burned brighter and hotter than any female he had ever been with.

Areana should be arriving at Tyre in a day or two, which was only about two days away of easy riding. But why waste the time when he could be there in less than half an hour?

With his father gone on his tour, Navuh could take the flyer with none any the wiser.

He could spend the night with her and be back by sunrise.

The flyer's mechanics were already under compulsion not to reveal his air travels, and his servants knew not to ask questions. As far as they were concerned, he was visiting a lover, which was actually true, except for the identity of his mystery woman, which he hoped no one suspected.

Until he had to deliver the flyer to his father, Navuh could be spending each night with Areana. Regrettably, he would have to come back to court each morning.

Was it risky?

Definitely.

Was it out of his character to take unnecessary risks?

That depended on the definition of necessary, and the blurry line between necessary and desirable.

Ruling over the entire civilized world could not be defined as necessary, but it was desirable in the same way that having Areana was. Both filled him with a sense of purpose and elation.

Which meant that he was losing his mind, or had lost it already. Having a woman, any woman, could not come close to him sitting on Ahn's throne.

In his quarters, Navuh removed his cloak and tossed it on a chair. "Please draw me a bath," he told his servant.

"Of course, my lord."

When the tub was ready, Navuh dismissed his manservant, took off the rest of his clothes, and got in. Fully submerged in the water, he let the heat radiate through his tense muscles.

So far, things were going according to plan, but since everything had been rushed because of Areana's impending arrival at court, there were some crucial details he still needed to work out.

Navuh did not like half-baked plans.

Hence the stress and mental fatigue.

As long as Mortdh was away, Areana was safe. But what was he going to do upon his father's return?

It would take the compelled warriors at least ten days to deliver their eyewitness murder testimony to Ahn, and then a few more days until Mortdh was summoned to appear before the council, which he might refuse to do.

Sentencing could be passed in his absence, but then it was anyone's guess how long it would take for the council's delegation to come and arrest Mortdh. The entire process could take a couple of moon cycles. Maybe even more if Ahn's council of gods deliberated for days on end.

In the meantime, Mortdh might decide to take out his anger on Areana, or use her as a bargaining chip against her father.

Bottom line, Areana had to disappear. Which meant that Navuh had to stash her somewhere until Mortdh was taken care of, and it was safe for her to arrive at court.

Hopefully, she had been smart enough to keep a low profile and not advertise her presence. Then again, she was traveling with a contingent of Ahn's uniformed warriors. People would notice.

There was no clean and easy solution to this. Whatever he came up with was not going to be fail-proof.

The only explanation he could offer his father for her disappearance was a bandit attack. Except, Mortdh's territory was free of them, and Tyre was part of it.

He would have to intercept Areana before she arrived at the city, bring disguises for her and her men, and then sneak her into Tyre and hide her there.

His mother's old house would be perfect for that, but it would also be the most damming for him if Areana's whereabouts were discovered.

Still, he could not think of a better hiding place. Since his mother's premature death, the house had stood empty for decades. Navuh had taken care of it, hiring a cleaning lady to tidy up every couple of moon cycles, and inspecting the property at least once a year for damages. The place had a tall fence, was furnished, and everything was in good working condition. It could comfortably accommodate Areana and her entourage.

37

AREANA

*S*ea breeze caressed Areana's skin as Tula lifted both of the wagon's flaps. "We can look at the water while we wait for the captain to return. I like watching the seagulls and listening to their cries."

Areana adjusted the pillow at her back. "I thought you did not like the sea."

"I do not like going into the water, but I like everything else. I even like the fishy smell." Tula sat cross-legged on the floor pillow. "I hope the captain finds us an inn."

"I doubt it. This is just a small fishing village, not a real town."

Still, camping out on the beach was a big improvement over camping out in the desert. To start with, it was much cooler, and dipping in seawater was refreshing after a long day of travel. A bath was better, but in the absence of one, even salty seawater was welcome.

The captain returned from his tour in less than half an hour. "I am sorry, my lady, but this town does not have an inn. I was lucky to find a store to replenish our supplies."

"It was worth a try." She smiled at him. "I guess it is camping for tonight."

He bowed. "Yes, my lady."

The men were well practiced in erecting the camp each night and dismantling it each morning. In less than an hour, the animals were taken care of, grazing on a green patch of growth, Areana's tent was up, and the cook was halfway done with preparing their evening meal.

All in all life on the road was not bad.

Or perhaps Areana had just gotten used to it. This was her new reality—an in-between state that she was in no hurry to end. As long as she was on the road, she did not need to face Mortdh or anyone else at his court.

She had no illusions as to the welcome she was about to receive from his concubines or even his servants. Everyone was going to treat her with suspicion and hostility.

Except for Navuh. He was friendly toward her, and they had shared intimacy, so maybe she could count him as an ally, but she did not really know him.

Unlike the gods who had tried to court her after Ahnon's death, Navuh did not talk about himself. He was cloaked in mystery, which was no doubt part of the attraction.

On the one hand, Areana was curious and wanted to find out more about the man, but on the other hand, she was scared of what she was going to find out. Most people made an effort to portray themselves in the best possible light, but once the thin layer of pretense was scratched, all kinds of nasty things were revealed.

"Dinner is ready, my lady," Tula said. "Would you like to eat in your tent or outside with the men?"

Areana pushed up to her feet. "I will eat outside."

It was not proper etiquette for a goddess to dine with

her guards, but Areana no longer cared for such trivialities. While on the road, rules could be bent, or even broken.

Tula carried out a small stool for Areana to sit on, and then brought her a loaded plate. "Wine or water, my lady?"

"Water, please."

When she was done pouring, Tula straightened up. "Look at this poor man." She pointed at a figure approaching from further down the beach. "He is carrying such a huge sack on his back, and he is limping."

As they watched the man get closer, the captain put his plate down and lifted his sword. The other guards followed.

"He is just one lame man." Areana waved a dismissive hand. "You can put down your weapons and resume eating."

"It might be a disguise, my lady. And this man might be an assassin sent to do you harm. I am not taking chances with your safety."

She laughed. "I am a goddess. What could a single male, human or immortal, manage to do?"

The captain shook his head. "I have heard rumors that Mortdh is training warriors to block their minds against thralling. And some people are just naturally immune. None of your tricks might work on him."

"Still, he would have to get close enough to me to do anything, and I have you to protect me."

The captain smirked and lifted his sword. "Exactly, my lady."

With everyone on alert, Areana did not feel right being the only one eating and put her plate down as well. Instead, she focused on the lone figure getting closer and strained her eyes to see his face. Something about the man's clothes looked familiar, especially the way his head cover was loose and hiding his face.

Could it be Navuh?

Not likely. Navuh would not have carried a huge sack on his back as part of his disguise. There was no need to go to such extremes. The commoner garb and the head cover were enough. Besides, Navuh's style was sneaking in at night and not making his approach visible from afar.

So why was her heart beating frantically against her ribcage? Did it know something her mind did not?

"Stop right there!" the captain commanded when the man had shuffled all the way up to their campsite. "And drop your sack on the ground."

"That will not be necessary," a familiar voice said. "Lady Areana is expecting me, and I come bearing gifts."

With a mixture of excitement and curiosity, Areana watched the captain let Navuh through.

It struck her as strange that her guards responded to Navuh's commands as if he were their lord. Ahn's warriors should have perceived him as an enemy, and not a trusted friend of their lady who could come and go as he pleased. But maybe they were taking their cues from her.

After all, she had welcomed Navuh every time he had come visiting.

38

NAVUH

"*W*hat do you have in there?" Areana asked when they got inside her tent.

"Disguises." Navuh loosened the top knot of his sack and spilled its contents on the tent floor.

She eyed the pile and grimaced. "What for?"

"I will tell you all about it after this." He pulled her into his arms and smashed his lips against hers.

Wrapping her arms around his neck, Areana melted into his body, kissing him back with just as much fervor. "I missed you," she whispered when they came up for air.

"You forgot to cast a silencing shroud."

"Right." She waved her hand.

Compared to Mortdh's, Areana's shroud was sloppy and incomplete, but it was better than nothing.

"I missed you too." He smoothed his hands over her silky hair, then cupped her cheeks and kissed her again. "I cannot get enough of you."

When he reached for the straps holding her dress up and started pulling them down, Areana put a hand on his chest. "We cannot. Tula might come in."

"I told her I needed to talk to you in private."

Areana chuckled. "And you think she listened? She will wait for a little while and then come in to ask if we need anything to drink or eat."

"She will not come in. People do not disobey my orders." Especially when imbued with compulsion.

"Oh, really?" Areana arched a brow. "Never?"

"Never."

"You are very sure about that."

"I am."

Taking his hand, she led him behind the privacy partition, where a washbowl and several washrags rested on a short stool. "In case you are wrong, we will at least have a moment's notice."

Frantic with need, they tore at each other's clothes, nearly ripping them apart in their hurry to be skin to skin.

Too impatient for prolonged preparations, he took her down on the tent floor and entered her with one brutal thrust.

Eyes glowing with pale blue light, Areana gasped and arched up, taking him even deeper.

Thank the Fates, she was just as desperate for him as he was for her, and already wet when he entered her. He did not want to hurt her, not like that.

Pain could be part of pleasure, but it required a different mindset.

Tonight, their coming together was about basic coupling, not about sexual games. Those would come later.

Provided everything went according to plan.

Fast and rough, their lovemaking was a dance of entangled limbs, searching mouths, and nipping teeth. He almost climaxed when Areana's small fangs pierced the skin of his shoulder, holding back the eruption with all the willpower he could muster.

Her fingernails scored grooves of fire on his back as his fangs popped through her skin. He did not keep still for the bite. Holding her pinned down with his fangs clamped on her neck, he kept plunging into her until the explosion came, blackening his vision.

When it was over, guilt and regret assailed him when he saw the damage he had done to her neck. It looked as if Areana had been mauled by a beast, which was not far from the truth.

He had lost control.

Licking the wound, he kept at it until no trace of it remained. When he was done tending to her neck, he pulled out and reached for one of the washrags.

"I am sorry for hurting you," Navuh said as he rubbed her inner thighs with the cloth. "It was not my intention. I got carried away." He dipped the rag in the washbasin and pressed it gently to her core.

Reaching with her fingers for the spot he had so savagely bitten, Areana patted around. "It hurt, but not terribly. And now it is gone."

It was fortunate she had not seen her neck right after his brutal attack. She might have never wanted to join with him again.

"I am glad I did not hurt you too badly." Navuh handed Areana her dress.

Once they were both clothed, he offered her a hand up and led her to the seating area. "You wanted to know what the disguises are for."

"Yes." She poured water into a goblet and handed it to him, then poured some for herself.

"In a couple of days, you are going to reach Tyre, which is in Mortdh's territory. I do not want anyone to know you have arrived. Therefore, your warriors will need to be dressed as regular caravan guards, and you will need to be dressed as a high-born human lady and pretend to be one."

He lifted a dark-haired wig and a bag filled with small jars of various face paints. "You will have to put the wig on and smear every exposed part of your body with the face paint. Hopefully, it will cover not only your pale skin but also your glow. To be safe, however, you should stay out of sight as much as possible and hide your body under clothing."

Areana emptied the goblet before putting it down. "Why?"

"I want to hide you from my father. I cannot stand the thought of him putting his hands on you. Especially not now when he is in one of his foul moods. When you do not show up, I will pretend to investigate and then report to him that I cannot find you. I will suggest that you must have fallen victim to a bandit attack."

"Is he going to buy it?"

"I do not know. He might think that you have escaped or that you are hiding."

"And where would I hide? I have nowhere to go."

"I have a house in Tyre you can hide in. I know it is not ideal, and that you will be trapped inside of it, but it is not much different from being trapped in the harem. Just not as luxurious. Not that it is a hovel. It is furnished and in good condition. There is room for you and your guard, and it has a big fenced-in yard to store the wagons and animals in."

Areana narrowed her eyes. "Does your father know about the house?"

"Yes. It used to belong to my mother. He bought it for her, and I inherited it when she died."

"Your mother was a human?"

He nodded. "She was the chief priestess in one of Mortdh's temples, too important and prominent to be taken into his harem. That was why he bought her the house." And because she was the only one who had given him a son, and for a while Mortdh had hoped for more.

Areana reached for his hand. "When did she die? Was it recently?"

"I was twelve when she died. It was a simple human disease my father could have cured with a tiny bit of his blood. But he did not."

"I am surprised that you know about this. This is the gods' most highly guarded secret. Still, if he loved her, he would have done it for her. Maybe even without her knowledge."

"He had tired of her long before she got sick, and he could not care less whether she lived or died. He was only interested in me."

Navuh's fingers closed around the goblet, squeezing the metal until it groaned under the pressure. "It took me four days to climb up to his mountain stronghold and beg him to help my mother. He looked so sincere when he told me that there was nothing he could do, and I believed him. When she died, he sent for me and pretended to be saddened by her death. I did not know back then that he could have saved her with minimal effort, so I believed his sad face and counted myself lucky for having the god take me in. I only learned the truth years later."

"Is that why you hate him?"

"Is it not reason enough?"

Areana chuckled sadly. "It is. We both have terrible fathers. Mine ignored me throughout my life, pretending I did not exist until he needed me for something. At least yours appreciates you."

Because I am the only son he actually fathered.

"I made myself useful. Otherwise, I would have been just another immortal warrior in his army."

Gently prying his fingers open, Areana took the goblet out of his hand and refilled it with water. "I understand what you are trying to do and why, but your plan is too risky. If your father suspects anything, he will search the house. And if the rumors I have heard are correct, he will not hesitate to execute you and probably me as well."

She was not wrong.

He was tempted to tell her the truth, but that was even riskier. "I wish I could hide you forever, but you are right. I will wait for his mood to improve and come get you when it does."

"What are you going to tell him in the meantime? Eventually, he will ask about me."

"I will think of a story. Many things can happen to a caravan. Anything from your animals contracting a disease and dying, to a broken wagon wheel. Or your little maid running away and you looking for her for days."

She laughed. "You have quite an imagination."

"It is a survival skill."

"But how can you lie to Mortdh? He is such a powerful god. Does he not smell the lies on you?"

"It is another survival skill. I learned how to block my mind and not allow him access to anything I do not want him to see, and I also learned how to control the scents I emit." He took her hand and gave it a light squeeze. "It seems that you are the only one who can make me lose control."

She smiled, her eyes sparkling with what he hoped was love. "That is because deep down you know you are safe with me. I will never betray your trust."

39

AREANA

*D*ark rain clouds blocked the sun as Areana stepped out of the house and into the garden, a basket with her embroidery under one arm and a bowl of cut fruit under the other.

With the tall walls surrounding Navuh's property providing plenty of privacy, she was spending as much of her time as she could out in the garden. Her soldiers had built a partition to separate the property into two areas. One side was dedicated to the animals and the smaller one for her use. The house was in between.

She liked horses, and did not mind patting their necks when they demanded her attention, but enduring the smell of their muck was another thing.

"I am going to the market," Tula said from the open door. "Is there anything you require, my lady?"

"See if you can find a nice aromatic soap. We are running low."

"I will." The girl offered her a quick curtsy.

They had been working on Tula's manners and a vocabulary appropriate for court.

Everyone had gotten used to Navuh's nearly nightly visits, but curiously no one was raising a brow at him staying in her room overnight. Not even Tula, who usually had no qualms about asking the most inappropriate questions and voicing her opinion about matters that were none of her business. Instead, the only thing the girl asked Navuh every time she saw him was whether her sister had arrived at Mortdh's court.

It seemed that poor Tula had been mistaken in assuming that Gulan had headed north.

Navuh had some strange power over her people. Were they afraid of him? Was his leadership ability so strong that no one questioned his commands?

Whatever it was, Areana was thankful for it. Every day she got to spend in Tyre with Navuh was a reason to celebrate. Who knew how many more of those happy days she would have?

Navuh was still claiming that his father was in a raging mood, and that it was better for her to stay away. But the thing was, yesterday Tula had brought news from the market that made Areana wonder whether Navuh was telling her the truth.

The girl had heard that Mortdh was touring his region and was away from his mountaintop palace.

It might have been an idle rumor, or an old one. Because there was no reason for Navuh to lie to her about that.

Unless he had made the whole thing up because he wanted her to himself and did not want her to arrive at his father's court.

But if that was so, why not just tell her?

Except, now that she thought of it, he had told her exactly that.

Navuh had said that he wanted to hide her from his

father because he could not stand the thought of Mortdh putting his hands on her. He had only added the comment about his father's bad mood as an afterthought.

Lifting her eyes to the sky, Areana willed the sun to go down faster. She could not wait for Navuh to arrive, and not only because she had questions.

The truth was that she was getting addicted to him, and as much as this could pose a problem in case she had to tolerate Mortdh's touch, Areana could not bring herself to regret any of it. Especially since Navuh seemed just as obsessed with her as she was with him.

How could it have happened so fast, though?

She did not love him, at least not in the same way she had loved Ahnon. What she felt for Navuh was more carnal in nature, and there was a certain affinity between them because both of them had shitty fathers. That was not love, though, and in the absence of love, addiction should not have set in so quickly.

Looking down at her embroidery, she realized that it was nearly complete. Only a finger-width of unadorned black ribbon remained. If she so wished, she could present it to Navuh tonight.

A thank-you gift for all his help.

When the last stitch was done, she lifted the long swath of fabric and examined her handiwork. It was beautiful. She could imagine Navuh wearing a tunic with her ribbon adorning it. He would look so handsome in it.

Every time he wore it, he would think of her.

With a sigh, Areana rolled the ribbon into a tight bundle and secured it with a piece of gold thread.

The question was whether the thought of her would bring Navuh happiness or pain once she became Mortdh's.

40

NAVUH

*N*avuh landed the flyer behind a hill overlooking Tyre and started the trek down to his house.

If he were inclined to indulge in wishful thinking, Navuh would have called it his and Areana's house. But, of course, it was not so.

Tonight could be the last they spent together for a while.

If everything went well, tomorrow he was going to deliver the flyer to his father, then spend the night in Mortdh's tent waiting for him to return after killing Khiann. Then he would take the flyer back to the palace, and Mortdh would continue his tour as if nothing had happened.

In that scenario, Navuh would only have to miss one night with Areana.

But if something went wrong, and Mortdh failed in his assassination attempt, or some other unforeseen event caused his father to end his tour and take the flyer home, then visiting Areana would not be possible until Navuh came up with an alternative plan.

Except, this portion of the plan should go smoothly, and he was not worried about it as much as the second part. Mortdh might decide to kill the warriors to eliminate all possible witnesses, and then he would not get arrested by the council or sentenced to entombment.

If that happened, Navuh would have to kill him himself. Which meant tampering with the flyer and causing Mortdh to crash.

It could take weeks, or even several moon cycles until Mortdh decided to fly somewhere. And in the meantime, it would be too dangerous for Navuh to visit Areana.

Not only that, he would have no choice but to either bring her to court or bring proof of her death to Mortdh.

Navuh shook his head. His own behavior baffled him. After so many years of meticulous planning, he was risking everything for a female.

He must have lost his mind, or perhaps Areana had charmed him with the help of magic.

But since Navuh did not believe in the supernatural, he had to take full responsibility for his actions. If things went wrong, he would have nothing else to blame but his own weakness.

No female was worth such great sacrifice. Not even a goddess. Except, he knew it for the lie it was. Logic and calculation did not apply to Areana and his insatiable craving for her.

As he reached the house, Areana's guards did not stop him even though he was wearing a disguise. By now, they recognized him even when he limped or walked hunched over.

"Good evening, my lord." The guard at the gate bowed and opened it for him.

"Good evening to you too, Bashun."

Every visit Navuh had been adding a little more

compulsion to the mind of whoever was standing guard at the time, not only to keep them from talking about Areana and his visits, but also to refrain from even questioning what was going on, or remembering that they should have headed back home weeks ago.

In their minds, the warriors' lives were all about guarding Areana and obeying Navuh's commands. The soldiers no longer answered to Ahn. They answered to Navuh.

It was not much different from what he was doing with his father's army. It was a slow process—one that could go much faster once Mortdh was out of the picture.

Surprisingly, the young maid had been the hardest to compel. She was strong-minded and opinionated and generally not as respectful as a maid should be, but he could not help but like her.

Perhaps the soldiers were easier because they had been trained to obey orders.

Little by little, though, he was taking control of Tula's mind as well. She was still asking about her sister, which was annoying since no one of that description had arrived at court, but he was working on that as well. Not wanting to turn the girl's brain into mush, he was careful to trickle the suggestion to forget her sister a little at a time.

"Navuh!" Areana ran up to him and wrapped her arms around his neck. "I thought you were not coming tonight."

He kissed her, and then gently pried her arms from around his neck. "I come whenever I can. It is not always possible." He took her hand and led her to her bedroom.

Even with the compulsion, public displays of affection made him nervous.

"Wait." She pulled her hand out of his grasp. "I have something for you."

He arched a brow as she reached for her embroidery

basket and tucked it under her arm. "Now we can go to my bedchamber." She threaded her arm through his.

"I made you a gift," Areana said as he closed the door behind them. "I hope you like it." She pulled a rolled up ribbon out of the basket. "It is not much, but it would look beautiful on a black tunic."

With deft fingers, she opened the knot holding the ribbon rolled up, and then unfurled it with a flick of her wrist.

The entire length was embroidered with gold thread, the precise stitches forming intricate geometric patterns. It must have taken many hours to make.

What did the gift symbolize, though?

He was at a loss.

Was it a gift of love?

A gift of gratitude?

He lifted the ribbon and smoothed his palm over it. "It is beautiful. Thank you."

Areana smiled apologetically. "I needed to fill my time with something. I know that painting or poetry are considered more appropriate pastimes for a goddess, but it was not feasible in a bumpy wagon. Besides, I like embroidery, and I like the idea of you wearing something that I made for you and thinking of me whenever you do."

He pulled her into his arms and kissed her hard. "First thing tomorrow morning, I will have my seamstress sew it onto a new tunic. In fact, I will ask her to make me several tunics and to use the ribbon only around the collar so I will have enough for every day of the week. I will never wear anything else."

The sudden burst in Areana's glow was the best indicator that he had pleased her with his words.

"I am so glad you like it. I was afraid you would think

my gift was inappropriate. Would you have preferred a poem? Or a painting?"

"Definitely not. After all, I cannot wear a painting, and if I wrote your poem on my chest, people would think that I had lost my mind." He kissed her again. "This is perfect."

Areana laughed, the heavenly sound sending goose bumps up his arms. Navuh wished he could make her laugh more often, but he was not a humorous man. Except, he could apparently make her glow.

With each visit, she glowed more brightly. He had lit the spark that had been dimmed for so long. Now it illuminated her from the inside, and it was getting stronger by the day.

Or rather by the night.

He could not remember whether Areana had shone so brightly when her mate had been still alive. Perhaps the spark he had lit was burning stronger than the one her mate had ignited.

Did Areana love him?

Or was it only about the great sex they shared?

Did he love her?

The only love Navuh had ever known had been his mother's, and it had died along with her. He was unfamiliar with romantic love. Perhaps it was right there in front of him, but he did not recognize it for what it was?

It was on the tip of his tongue to ask Areana if she loved him, but he stifled the impulse.

Whatever she felt for him could not compare to the love she had felt for her mate, and he would rather not hear her say so.

What they had was an attraction, and he should not confuse lust with love.

He could never win her heart because it was impossible

to fight a loving memory that had probably been turned into a shrine of worship for her dead mate.

Besides, even a weak goddess like Areana would never see Navuh as more than a lowly immortal—good enough for a lover but never good enough for an official mate.

That was until he took over his father's territory and eventually the entire civilized world. Then no one would ever look down on him again.

Right now, Areana's main objective was to avoid mating Mortdh, and that was all. Just like other females, she thought to use him to advance her own agenda. The only difference was that he had fallen for her act. She almost had him convinced with a gift that she must have worked on for many days. But it had been just another trick in the arsenal of feminine wiles she used to gain influence and protection from a powerful ally.

One of the first things his father had drilled into his head was that a powerful male should never allow himself to be weakened by a female. Mortdh's insanity did not make his father stupid, and Navuh had internalized many of the lessons he had been taught.

Women were manipulative creatures and used their charms to get what they wanted out of men. Stupid males bought the act and became slaves to their mates' and lovers' whims. The smart ones knew not to get emotionally involved and used females for what they were meant for—sex and breeding.

Somewhere in the back of his head, a small voice was whispering that he was telling himself falsehoods because he was suddenly terrified of losing his soul to this woman. But Navuh stifled that voice, allowing the anger and hatred that had been the primary drivers behind his ambition to take over.

41

AREANA

"*I* am so glad you like it." Areana took the ribbon from Navuh's hands, rolled it into a tight bundle, and secured it with a piece of gold thread.

"Do you know what I like even more?" His dark eyes narrowed into slits.

Lifting her eyes to the ceiling, she pretended to think it through. "Me?"

"You are getting closer." For some reason, he seemed irritated by her answer.

"Naked in bed?"

"That is the correct answer."

Areana was confused. The words were part of their normal banter, but Navuh's tone and expression did not match them in spirit. He seemed reserved, even brooding.

Instinctively, Areana took a step back. "What is wrong?"

"You are still dressed." Navuh crossed his arms over his chest and glared at her.

Was it part of some sex game he was playing with her?

That was the only explanation that made sense to her.

A couple of moments ago he had seemed so happy with her gift, and nothing had happened between then and now to affect his mood negatively.

Unless, and this was a very disconcerting thought, the son had inherited his father's insanity, and she was now witnessing its first signs.

"Remember what I told you about obedience?" He advanced on her, gripping her exposed shoulders. "When I tell you to strip, I expect you to respond immediately." His tone was calm and measured, not angry, and his palms were gentle and warm on her skin as he slowly slid the straps down her arms.

It was a game after all.

Areana released a relieved breath. "My apologies, my lord. I will do better in the future." She let the loose gown drop to the floor and then stepped out of it.

Nude before him, she waited for his next command.

"On your knees, Areana."

Fates, to do as he commanded felt terribly awkward, but also arousing. Areana dropped to her knees and looked up at Navuh's austerely beautiful face, checking his response to her immediate compliance.

He cupped her cheek and smiled. "Very good. You are learning."

Slowly, as if he had all the time in the world, Navuh took off his tunic, folded it and put it on top of a chair. He then removed his pants and folded them too, all along watching her waiting obediently on her knees.

Proudly nude, he palmed his erection and brushed the swollen head over her lips, fisting her hair with his other hand to hold her in place. "Open for me, Areana."

Unsure whether she liked this game or not, Areana did as she was told. Did he expect her to know what to do?

Because she did not. It should not be too difficult to figure out, but she did not want to displease him by doing something wrong.

He pushed just the tip into her mouth. "Use your tongue, Areana. Lick it."

Apparently, he was aware of her inexperience in this form of pleasuring a male and was giving her instructions, which was good.

She did not want to disappoint him.

Navuh had been very generous, pleasuring her with his mouth almost every time they were intimate. She wanted to return the favor and do it well, not fumble like a novice.

When he pushed a little deeper, she trailed her hands up his strong thighs and gripped his length, seeking to control his forward movement, but he removed her hand and gripped her jaw.

"No hands, Areana."

He wanted her at his mercy, and for some reason, it excited her. Closing her eyes, she relaxed, submitting to whatever he wanted to do with her.

Pulling on her hair, he forced her to tilt her head up. "Eyes on me, Areana."

As she did, the lustful dark look on Navuh's face had her core convulse with need, and an outpour of moisture coated her thighs.

Why did it excite her so? Was it his commanding tone? Or was it the way he was holding her, the tight grip of his fingers on her jaw, the pressure on her scalp from where he was fisting her hair?

Then he began to thrust, shallow and short jabs until she adjusted to the rhythm and relaxed in his hold, then a little deeper and longer, until he was hitting the back of her throat and she gagged.

He withdrew all the way, letting her catch her breath before pushing back inside and starting all over. His hands never relaxing their grip on her, he repeated the same sequence of short and shallow to begin with, then following with long and hard ones until she took him all the way down without gagging.

"Good girl," he praised. "Do not worry. I am not going to ejaculate in your mouth this time, not on your maiden voyage."

Doing all she could to take him without gagging, her eyes tearing from the effort, she had not even considered that.

She would have gagged for sure.

And yet, Areana could not help but get even more aroused imagining him spouting his essence into her mouth. Clutching his muscular bottom, she spurred him on to do just that.

Except, Navuh had different ideas. Pulling all the way out, he bent and lifted her by the waist, then tossed her face down on the bed. A split moment later he was behind her, pulling her bottom up and spearing into her.

It was as if his shaft had sprung free the coil that had been tightening inside her. As soon as he hit the mouth of her womb, Areana threw her head back and cried out her climax.

Gripping her hips with bruising force, Navuh pounded into her with a punishing rhythm, his groin slamming into her bottom on every forward thrust.

There was nothing affectionate or even intimate about their coupling. Navuh was fucking her like an animal, and she was loving it.

As he shouted his release, she orgasmed again. A moment later his sharp fangs pierced the skin of her neck, and yet another climax exploded out of her. Then the venom hit her system, triggering a long chain of smaller explosions.

Overwhelmed and blissed out, Areana blacked out.

NAVUH

*A*s Navuh entered his quarters, the three warriors he had handpicked to accompany Mortdh were already waiting for him in the antechamber to his office.

Leaping to attention, the three bowed.

"Greetings, my lord," Mahog said first.

His comrades hastily repeated his words.

"Greetings, warriors. Follow me." Navuh pushed open the door to his reception chamber and walked in.

As the three entered, once again standing to attention, Navuh cast a silencing shroud. Usually he did not bother because it was effective only against humans, but under the circumstances, every precaution had to be taken.

His wing in Mortdh's stronghold had undergone special improvements. All the walls had been doubled, with the air gap between them ensuring excellent sound-proofing. On top of that, his reception chamber was the innermost room in his quarters, and no one other than his compelled to loyalty manservant was allowed anywhere near it while Navuh was holding meetings in there.

"At ease, soldiers. Please, take a seat." He motioned to the two divans.

He had been working with each of them individually, first to gauge their susceptibility to compulsion, and then reinforcing their loyalty to him, and only him. For the last several days, he had started pushing the script he had prepared into their minds.

Leaning against his desk, he snapped his fingers. "Look into my eyes while you listen to my words." He pushed a little compulsion.

It was important not to overdo it. He could not deliver them to his father with eyes glazed and mouths drooling. They needed to appear completely normal.

"You are going with Lord Mortdh on a mission of vengeance against Lord Ahn and Princess Annani. To restore his honor, Lord Mortdh is going to kill the usurper who stole his intended. You are going to assist him by eliminating the usurper's guards. You are elite warriors, and you have the element of surprise on your side. I trust that you can defend Lord Mortdh."

The three nodded.

That had been the easy part, which did not require any mind manipulation.

The second part, the one about going to Ahn and confessing the crime, was trickier.

Because of the suggestive nature of compulsion, the men were going to repeat what he had told them to say word for word, which meant that he had to stage the fight in his head and supply all the details. Navuh could leave nothing to their own imaginations or interpretations, or expect them to deliver more information, because they were not going to.

They would tell Ahn and the council only the exact words he had planted in their heads, and in the precise sequence. That was why Navuh had it written down and had been repeating it word for word each time.

It was a breach in his own safety protocol—Navuh never wrote down anything that could be used to incriminate him—but since even a few misplaced words had the potential to ruin everything, he had no choice.

Once this last session was over, he was going to burn the parchment. By now, he had it memorized, but it was a shame he could not keep it as a memento. The killing scene he had concocted was deviously brutal and vicious. He had to ensure that upon hearing the testimony the council would unanimously sentence Mortdh to entombment.

With such damming evidence, not even Ekin, Mortdh's own father, would be able to vote against the sentence.

"Mahog, repeat to me everything that you are going to tell Ahn's council of gods."

The soldier sounded somewhat rehearsed, but that was all right. The council would attribute his stiff delivery to nervousness.

He had the other two retell the fabricated story as well.

"That will do. Meet me at the flyer hangar in two hours. Until then, eat, rest, and do not breathe a word of what we have talked about in here to anyone, not even among yourselves."

GULAN

"*I* can smell the sea," Gulan said.

Shever leaned forward and strained his old eyes. "I cannot see the town yet, but I can tell we are getting close. Back and forth I have traveled this trail many times. I can do it with my eyes closed."

The wagon driver had become a good friend to her during the long days of travel, or rather to Vodag, the young immortal male she pretended to be. They made a good team, and the tall tales of his youthful shenanigans had helped alleviate the boredom as well as dim the pain in her chest.

Esag's memory still squeezed at her heart, but it no longer brought tears to her eyes.

Talking with Shever about it had helped.

When he had asked what a young immortal was doing as a lowly laborer on a caravan, she had told him her story, just in reverse.

Vodag was in love with a girl who was promised to another. When the girl refused to break her engagement,

Vodag's heart broke, and he ran away to avoid seeing his beloved join with another.

"There are plenty of fish in the sea," Shever had told her. "You will fall in love again, maybe more than once, maybe even many times, and each time you will think that she is the one. Young hearts are like that—tempted by the promise of love and not very choosy."

"So how do you know which one is your truelove?" Gulan had asked.

"You do not. And it is not important. If you find a good woman, who will bear your children and take care of you, count yourself lucky." He had shaken his head. "But if you are unlucky, you might get tempted by a pretty face and end up with a shrew who will make your life miserable. Who knows? Maybe you are better off without that girl. Did she have a pretty face?"

"Very."

"She might have been a shrew."

"Just because she was pretty?"

"Pretty girls think too much of themselves."

Gulan wondered if it worked the same with handsome men. Esag was undoubtedly full of himself, cocky and flirty. He had been so surprised when she had refused his insulting proposal. He had expected her to be grateful for the crumbs he had thrown her way.

"The animals are sensing something. I hope it is not a sandstorm," Shever said.

While the horses seemed to want to rush forward, the donkeys pulling the wagons stopped in their tracks.

Something was definitely going on. "Is it common to have sandstorms so close to the sea?"

"Farther south, but not here."

As the animals grew more agitated by the second, the

people looked nervously around, searching for the disturbance coming their way.

Sandstorms were dangerous. They could bury the caravan and kill the humans as well as the animals. The few immortals would survive and might dig the others out, but that depended on how bad the storm was.

Except, it was not a sandstorm they should have worried about.

Suddenly, the earth started shaking. At first, it was not so bad, but it intensified in seconds. It seemed as if the desert floor was rolling in waves under them.

Gulan and Shever jumped down and unhitched the donkeys. The old human was not nearly strong enough to hold on to the panicked animals, so Gulan took the reins from him, trying to keep her footing on the moving earth under her while holding on to the four scared donkeys.

The other caravan drivers were doing the same, but with much less success. They did not have a strong immortal to help them, and several panicked animals galloped away.

It was getting worse, the shaking and rolling becoming more violent, but it did not deter Shever from rushing to help his friends at the wagon in front of them.

The earth groaned, the terrifying sound preceding a crack that immediately grew into a big chasm. For one panicked moment, Gulan watched in horror as it opened its big hungry mouth and swallowed the front wagon, including the men and the animals they had been holding.

Instinct more than thought propelling her to action, Gulan let go of the donkeys and leaped after her friend. Flattening herself on the chasm's lip, she caught Shever's wrist a split moment before he would have plunged to his death, and flung him up and away. The other man was clinging to a protruding rock, too far down for her to reach.

Gulan crawled closer, her entire upper body leaning over the edge.

"Reach for my hand!" she shouted.

"I cannot!"

"Reach! Or you are going to die! Now!"

Clinging to the rock with one hand, the man reached with the other. Their fingers were almost touching, but she could not grab a hold. Crawling a little closer, Gulan dug her toes into the shaking ground and stretched her arm.

As her fingers closed around the man's hand, she squeezed hard and hauled him up, then flung him to the side.

The animals were lost. But at least she had managed to save the two drivers.

Carefully, Gulan started crawling back, when Shever yelled, "Look out!"

A split second later a heavy weight smashed into her head, and then there was nothing.

44

MORTDH

*E*xcitement swirling in his gut, Mortdh lifted up to the skies and headed for the desert.

It had been so long since he had fought and killed. The last time he had spilled blood had been back on the home planet before his father, his uncle, and their sister had been charged with leading an expedition to mine for gold in the hellhole called earth.

It had not been as hot when they had first landed on the primitive planet, but even then it had been barely endurable for people who came from a cold, dark world.

The banishment had been called an expedition, but they had all known that it had been punishment for their respective roles in the civil unrest and later uprising.

His grandfather had gotten rid of his overly ambitious offspring, replacing them with his more manageable children, the ones he could control and who posed no threat to his rule.

It had been a brilliant move.

Gold was necessary for space travel and as a conductor in their devices. By putting his official successors in charge of the mission, he had appeared as the people's hero. Some might have suspected the real reason, but no one had cared as long as the shipments of gold had arrived on time.

Evidently, though, a different source for the precious metal had been found, or perhaps the scientists had found a different solution, because all contact had been severed thousands of years ago.

It suited Mortdh's agenda perfectly.

On the home world, he had been a nobody. On earth, he could become an omnipotent ruler like his grandfather.

First, he was going to kill the usurper and restore his honor, and as soon as his army was ready, he was going to charge the south and strip the other gods of their powers. They would either bow to him, or he would dispose of them one way or another.

As he reached the area where the caravan was supposed to be, Mortdh dropped to a lower altitude and scanned the desert for the row of wagons.

He wondered whether it was possible to take control of every human and immortal mind on that caravan from up high in the air. It would make things easier if the only one whose mind still functioned was the usurper.

It would be a unique pleasure to watch him tremble in fear as he anticipated his impending death by Mortdh's hand.

"I think I can see it, my lord." The warrior sitting next to him pointed with his finger.

Mortdh turned the flyer in the direction the immortal had indicated, and indeed there was a row of tiny shapes in the distance.

Blood rushing through his veins, Mortdh circled around and started his descent.

"Do not move until I tell you to," he ordered the

warriors. "And do not interfere unless one of the god's immortal guards comes to his defense."

He did not need help killing the young, inexperienced god. The warriors he had brought along were a precaution in case one or more of the merchant god's guards were naturally immune to mind control.

It was highly unlikely, but as Navuh had advised, it was better to come prepared.

"They must have heard the flyer's engine," one of the warriors sitting behind him said. "The caravan is not moving."

Mortdh frowned. The flyer made very little noise, and it was still too high up and far away even for the immortals accompanying the caravan to hear.

A moment later a loud boom revealed the real reason for the caravan's stop. Even from up high in the sky, Mortdh could see the earth roll in waves as if it was a stormy ocean and not solid land. A large crack started in the distance, zigzagging its way toward the caravan at a rapid speed and opening wider and wider as it progressed.

"Dear merciful Fates," the soldier beside him whispered. "They are all going to die."

They were going to die one way or another, but, regrettably, it was not going to be by his or his elite warriors' hands.

Hovering high above the ground, Mortdh watched as wagon after wagon fell into the deep chasm until not even one remained.

The fucking Fates had just robbed him of his chance for revenge.

The earth kept shaking, the zigzagging crack rushing across the land like a thunderbolt, until it was lost beyond the horizon.

Minutes seemed to last hours until the violent shaking

stopped and the crack closed upon itself, leaving only a thin jagged line on the ground.

Everything stilled.

His warriors barely breathed as they stared in shock at the barren land, where dozens of lives came to a violent end, including that of Annani's mate.

The usurper was a god and therefore could survive even being buried alive. Ahn's immortal warriors could as well. But unless someone found them and revived them, they would stay in the ground for eternity.

Taking his flyer further down, Mortdh circled the area two more times, making sure nothing remained above ground to indicate where the caravan was buried.

Satisfied that no one would ever know the exact location, Mortdh turned around and headed back home.

They could search for thousands of years, dig half of the desert up, and never find the caravan's burial ground.

45

NAVUH

*U*p north, in Mortdh's lavish tent, Navuh was not wasting time as he waited for his father's return.

Uncharacteristically, Mortdh had left his tablet behind, and in plain view. To be so careless, he must have been distracted by his bloodthirsty eagerness for the kill. The thing was password protected, but his father had not been very careful when he had tapped it in while Navuh had been watching.

It was a fascinating read, but not overly surprising.

As he had suspected, his father had only nominated Navuh as his second-in-command and successor as a temporary measure. Mortdh planned to replace him as soon as he fathered a full-blooded son with a goddess, and not just any goddess, but Ahn's favorite daughter and the heir to his throne—Annani.

The thing was, before gods started taking human lovers, creating the race of immortals, and before Mortdh moved up north to establish his own power base, he had bedded many of the goddesses. And yet, even though he had thousands of years to produce a child, none of the goddesses had given him one.

His father was just as infertile as the other gods, or even more so since he was one of the oldest and had had more time and opportunity than most.

He deluded himself if he thought that anything had changed in that regard. Even if Mortdh somehow managed to get Annani to mate with him, the union would not produce any children.

Navuh's position was secure.

If he were a believer, he would have credited the Fates with his father's lack of success in producing a pure-blooded heir. It was very tempting to believe that the purpose of their divine intervention was Navuh's rise to power.

Except, it no longer mattered.

Mortdh's days as the northern ruler were numbered. All Navuh had to do was bide his time until the warriors he had compelled reached Ahn and gave their testimony of Mortdh's crime.

The only hitch in his plan was Areana.

Until the council sent gods to arrest his father, there was still a chance that Mortdh might discover that Navuh had been hiding her. The consequences would be dire. Mortdh was not stupid and might figure out Navuh's plan. It would be too late for his father to save himself, but he might execute Navuh before the gods came for him.

He should have never allowed himself to get so carried away with the female.

On the other hand, if not for Areana, Navuh would have never come up with the fantastic plan of getting rid of Mortdh without dirtying his hands or tarnishing his reputation.

Outside, a horse neighed, stomping its hoofs, and a

moment later a slight tremor shook the tent. It was over in a matter of seconds, and the animal calmed down. With a shrug, Navuh opened his father's tablet and continued reading.

When the temperature in the tent dropped, and the northern mountain wind picked up like it always did this time of year at nightfall, Navuh closed the tablet, wiped the surface clean, and returned it to where Mortdh had left it.

He did not have to wait much longer for his father's return.

Mortdh strode into the tent, unbuckled his sword, and tossed it aside.

He did not look happy.

Navuh filled a goblet with wine and handed it to his father. "Was the mission successful?"

"The usurper is no more."

"Then it is a cause for celebration." Navuh poured wine into another goblet and lifted it for a salute.

Ignoring Navuh and his raised goblet, Mortdh threw his head back and emptied the goblet's contents down his throat. "I did not kill him. I was too late." He spat the words through gritted teeth and tossed the goblet across the tent.

Every muscle in Navuh's body went rigid. "What do you mean you were too late?"

Pivoting on his heel, Mortdh glared at him. "Did you not feel the earthquake?"

"It was only a slight tremor."

"Here, but it was much more than a tremor over there. From the air, it looked as if solid ground turned into stormy water and was rolling in big waves. Then it cleaved asunder and swallowed the caravan whole."

"Did anyone notice your flyer?"

Mortdh chuckled darkly. "They were too busy dying."

"The god and his immortal guards might have survived."

Dread swirled in Navuh's gut. His entire plan had just gone up in smoke. Mortdh had not killed Khiann, he would not get arrested by the council, and he would not be sentenced to entombment. Everything was back to where it had been before, and Navuh would have to bring Areana to his father.

The pain in his gut belied all the self-talk he had indulged in, in an effort to minimize her importance.

Without her, all his grandiose plans were worthless. Even if he succeeded in achieving everything he set out to, he would not be able to enjoy it.

Mortdh sat in his armchair, the same one Navuh had been sitting on before his father's arrival and reading the god's ramblings. "The earth closed over them. Without breathable air, they had to go into stasis, and no one is going to find them and revive them. They are as good as dead."

"Yes, you are probably right."

Mortdh waved a dismissive hand. "I know I am right. The question is whether I continue with this tour or head home. I no longer need a cover for something that I did not do. I did not cause the earthquake." He chuckled again. "Although we can spread a rumor that I did. The humans would believe anything."

An idea started brewing in Navuh's mind. "We can do that, but you have to wait until the news of what happened reaches the north. Because how were you supposed to know, right?"

Mortdh smoothed his hand over his beard. "True. And that means that I need to continue the tour as well. Once the news spreads, I will claim to have caused the earthquake to avenge my honor. The humans will believe it and worship me even more reverently. The beauty of it is that Ahn cannot dispute my claim because then he will have to admit that gods are not as omnipotent as he wants the humans to believe they are."

Navuh bowed. "Brilliant plan, Father."

"Indeed." It seemed like the god's mood had undergone a complete turnaround. He waved a dismissive hand. "We will talk about it at a later time. Right now you need to take the flyer and the warriors back to the palace."

"Yes, of course." Navuh bowed again. "I will come back in two days. Officially, this time. Hopefully, by then the news of the earthquake will start trickling in."

Mortdh lifted his tablet. "I am going to prepare a speech."

With another bow, Navuh covered his head with the headdress and stepped out of the tent.

As he saw it, he had two choices. One was to remove the compulsion he had placed on the warriors to report to Ahn, and then compel them never to say a word about it to anyone.

He would then bring Areana to the stronghold while his father was still touring, and everything would go back to normal.

Or, he could continue with his plan as if Mortdh had indeed committed the murder, and keep Areana for himself.

The warriors would tell the story he had compelled them to confess to despite it never happening. With three reliable witnesses all telling the same story, no one would believe Mortdh when he claimed he did not do it.

It was a difficult decision to make.

Option one was the safest, but it would cost him Areana. Perhaps it was for the better. If he was forced to give her up, maybe her hold over him would loosen over time.

The goddess had too much power over him, and Navuh did not like anyone having such power. As long as he felt nothing for anyone, he was nearly invincible.

Areana was his one and only weakness. The best way to deal with it was to cut it off, suffer through the pain for as long as it took, and eventually get over it.

Except, even though option two was fraught with risk, he knew he was going to choose it over the safer one, and not only because it gave him Areana. He could almost taste the power, imagine everyone bowing to him and worshiping him the way they worshiped Mortdh.

The smart way to go was to wait patiently for the right opportunity and tamper with Mortdh's flyer. But that would mean the destruction of the only working airboat in the Northern Territory.

And then there was Areana.

Could he really stomach Mortdh taking her? Even temporarily?

46

ANNANI

As an earth tremor shook the palace, Annani's Odus rushed to catch the flower-filled vases and other knickknacks that rattled and shook and were about to fall.

When the shaking stopped after a couple of minutes, Annani sighed. "Thank the merciful Fates it is over. I hate earthquakes."

Her new maid rushed in. "Are you all right, my lady? Are you hurt?"

Annani waved a dismissive hand. "Everything is all right. Nothing broke."

The last time the palace had experienced a tremor, broken shards of ceramic vases and basins had to be swept off the floors, and the walls had to be patched up. Compared to that one, this tremor had been mild.

"Oh, good." The maid wiped her sweaty hands on her tunic. "I will go back to preparing the basket for your evening meal with Lord Khiann."

"Thank you. When it is ready, please bring it to the airboats' enclosure."

"Of course, my lady."

Hopefully, Khiann and his caravan were all right. Since most quakes happened across the gulf to the east, and Khiann had taken his caravan in the opposite direction heading west, he had probably felt nothing.

Still, she would rather see that with her own eyes.

"Okidu, go find Onidu and Oridu. We are leaving as soon as Musha is finished with the basket."

Her mechanical servant tilted his head, indicating miscomprehension.

With how lifelike the Odus seemed, Annani often forgot that they were unable to interpret instructions. They had to be told exactly what to do.

"In half an hour, meet me next to the airboat, and bring Onidu and Oridu with you."

"As you wish, mistress." He bowed.

Once the door closed behind her servant, Annani took off her dress and put a comfortable tunic on, pairing it with a pair of loose pants. Next, she braided her long hair and tied a scarf around her face. Unlike a carriage, the airboat did not have a roof. Ekin had told her that it used to have a transparent canopy made from a resilient material, but it had crumbled with age, and they had nothing to replace it with.

In the airboats' enclosure, her Odus were waiting for her next to the smaller one of the two royal airboats parked there, the one Annani had appropriated for her use as soon as Ahn had taught her how to pilot it.

The big one belonged to Ahn, and another one just like it belonged to Ekin, but it was never there because his son Toven was constantly taking it to explore faraway lands.

Fortunately for Annani, her mother was terrified of heights, and her aunt Hattra—the only other royal family member—ruled over a city-state an hour's carriage ride away and never showed any interest in piloting an aircraft.

Which meant that Annani had the smaller craft all to herself.

By her estimate, Khiann should have reached the midpoint of his journey, which meant a little less than an hour's flight away. She should arrive just on time for the caravan crew to be done with setting up camp for the night.

Except, an hour and a half later, there was still no sign of his caravan.

Had she missed it somehow? The sun was setting, but it was not dark yet, and even if it were, she could see perfectly well with only the moon and stars for illumination.

"Look for the caravan," Annani told the Odus as she turned the airboat around. "It will look like small toy wagons from up here."

"Yes, mistress."

The longer she searched, the heavier the stone growing in her gut became. She circled around, orienting herself by recognizing familiar landmarks, and did another flyby.

Nothing.

When the sun set and there was no sign of campfires as far as her eyes could see, Annani started to fear the worst.

But what exactly should she fear?

The only thing that came to mind was the earthquake, but those were dangerous to people who were trapped in crumbling buildings, not to those out in the open, and not to gods and immortals.

Perhaps something else had happened?

What if the caravan had been attacked by bandits and they had killed the people and taken the wagons and animals away with them?

Frantically searching her mind for another logical explanation, something that would mean Khiann was all right, Annani circled the area once more. Eventually, though, she had no choice but to accept the inconceivable.

As she realized that bandits were the only possible explanation, a mournful sob escaped her throat and tears started running down her cheeks.

But Khiann could not be gone. They were soul mates. If he had died, she would have felt his soul leave his body and cross to the other side.

He must be alive.

Perhaps he had escaped and was hiding somewhere?

Wiping the tears away with a corner of her scarf, Annani brought her airboat lower and prepared to circle the area again and again until she found him.

"Look for a single man, not for wagons," she told the Odus.

"It is too dark to see, mistress," Okidu said.

She had not considered that the Odus' vision might not be as good as hers.

"I know. But master Khiann would know to light a torch."

She was clutching at straws, but there was nothing else she could do. To turn back would mean that she had given up, and Annani was not going to do so anytime soon.

Right now she was Khiann's only hope.

47

NAVUH

*D*espite Navuh's best efforts to stay away from Areana, as soon as the sun set he found himself sitting in the flyer's cockpit and turning the engine on.

It would have been prudent not to compound the risks he was taking for her, but he could not resist her pull. It was just too strong.

The warriors he had compelled were on their way to Ahn's capital, and his original plan was set in motion.

Last night, when he had dropped them off at the coastal city, he had reasoned that he could still change his mind any time before they reached their final destination, fly over and bring them back.

But if he did that, he would also have to pick Areana up and bring her to court. The guards could come with her maid and her things later.

That was what he should have done.

He still could.

No, he could not.

With a groan, Navuh punched the flyer's front panel. His father was right. Females were the bane of males' existence. He had never expected to risk not only his goals and aspirations, but also his very life for a woman—one who did not love him and never would.

Maybe that was the solution. If he made Areana hate him, she would push him away, and he would finally be free of her.

Except, it was idle talk unbefitting a smart man like him. He did not want to be free of her, and he did not want her to be free of him. What he wanted was to keep her locked up and ready to please him whenever he felt like having her. Not only that, he wanted her to accept that fate willingly. She could deny her love, but he would demand everything else she had to give.

That was it.

He just wanted to own a goddess and to get drunk on the power trip.

Except, that was a lie as well.

Owning any other goddess would have given him the sense of power he desired, but the idea did not stir his loins as owning Areana did.

Naturally, she would try to maneuver things around in a way that would allow her to preserve an illusion of independence. All she knew were Ahn's laws that favored females and sanctified their rights to choose their mates and own property and decide how they wanted to live their lives.

Perhaps, if she pleased him greatly, Navuh would allow her the illusion. If she did not, Areana would learn quite quickly that things were very different up north.

Yes, he would have her, but he would not allow her to manipulate him or influence his decisions as she had been doing since that day in Ahn's throne room.

Except, it was not her fault. It was his—Navuh was well aware of the fact—and he should remember to keep his anger directed where it belonged and not take it out on Areana.

She could not help being beautiful and gentle and all around perfect.

The last time they had been together, he had handled her too roughly. Navuh regretted getting carried away. Letting his anger instead of his mind dictate his actions was unacceptable—most unbecoming of a man who prided himself on his formidable brainpower and cool-headed approach.

That should never happen again.

Not that Areana had objected. Evidently, his darkness and dominance excited her. It was a common response, which was why he knew how easily things could get out of hand, especially with a female who embraced it.

To control others, a man had to be in control of himself first and accept responsibility for the well-being of those he expected to obey him. Which meant that even though Areana loved it rough, he should not oblige her too often, and especially not when his mood was dark.

Tonight, he was going to be gentle with her whether she wanted him to or not.

48

AREANA

*A*s Navuh entered the house, Areana ran up to him and threw her arms around his neck. "I am so glad you came." She buried her nose in his neck and inhaled his scent. "I missed you, and I was so worried."

Gently, he removed her arms and took a step back. "Why were you worried?"

His response reminded her that they were not alone, and that she was giving Tula and a roomful of warriors a show.

Her cheeks warming, she asked, "The earth tremor. Did you not feel it up in the mountains?"

He took her hand and led her outside to the backyard, where he sat on a bench and pulled her onto his lap. "It was a very mild earthquake. Were you frightened?"

"A few dishes fell off the table and broke, and Tula panicked. I had to hold her long after it was over. She is normally such a brave girl that it surprised me to see her so scared. Then she started talking about having a bad feeling that something terrible had happened, and I could not help but think about you and whether you were all right."

Caressing her back, Navuh pressed a soft kiss to her throat. "I am touched that out of all the people you could worry for, I was the only one you thought about."

With a sigh, she rested her cheek on his chest. "I did not realize it until you said it. But you were the only one for a reason. You are the dearest to my heart." This was as close to admitting her feelings for him as she dared to go.

Up until the earthquake, and her panic at the thought of something happening to him, Areana had thought that what she felt for Navuh was lust and gratitude for his help. But when faced with the possibility of losing him, she realized that her feelings ran much deeper than that.

Was it love? She was not sure, but it was close.

It did not make sense. She hardly knew him, and physical compatibility was not love. But it could be an addiction.

He kissed the top of her head. "It means a lot to me to hear you say that."

It did not escape her notice that he had not responded in kind. Was she just one of his many concubines? Not special in any way other than her being a goddess?

Eyes cast down, she blurted out her question. "Am I dear to you too? Or am I one more female you bed when you please?"

For several long moments he said nothing, his large hand still caressing her back, but then he lifted her hand to his lips and kissed it. "Since the first time we made love, I have not been with any other female."

It was not exactly a declaration of love, or even a promise of future fidelity, but it was better than nothing.

"I think I am getting addicted to you."

His hand on her back paused. "Is it not too soon? We have only been together for a short time. I have not bitten you enough times for you to get addicted to my venom."

Areana put her hand on his chest. "It is not only the venom I am addicted to. It is the whole package. I crave you constantly, and not only sexually. I just want to be with you, to hear your voice, to gaze at your handsome face, to look into your dark eyes and see the cunning intelligence in them."

Navuh cupped her cheek, his expression grave as he looked into her eyes. "Do not fall in love with me, Areana. I am not a good man."

He was not good, it was true, but he was not evil either. Except, she knew the potential to do great harm was there. If she were his, could she help steer him away from crossing the line?

"I am not falling in love with you."

"Good." The tinge of disappointment in his tone belied his reply.

"Maybe I can choose certain aspects of you to love. I can love your hands." She lifted one and kissed each finger. "I can love your hair." She loosened the tie holding it away from his face and smoothed her hand over the silky length. "And I can love your lips." She kissed his mouth.

"I can also love the way you pleasure me, your dominance and your generosity. I can love your intelligence and your levelheaded approach to problems. Should I continue?"

Areana had a feeling that Navuh's dark side was stronger than the good. He did not talk much about himself, but from the little he had told her, and what she knew about his father, it was clear that he was a product of his upbringing and his environment.

There were probably many things about Navuh that she would not like. But it did not matter. It was not as if she was deciding whether to choose him as her mate or not. They were both living on borrowed time, and as long as it lasted, they should enjoy each other.

Right now, sitting on his lap and wrapped in his arms, Areana was going to focus on the good, not the bad.

A rare smile brightened Navuh's dark features. "That could take all night, and I would rather spend it making love to you instead of talking about it."

49

NAVUH

*A*s Navuh landed the flyer in a clearing next to his father's encampment and started walking toward Mortdh's tent, the knot in his gut tightened the closer he got.

Had the summons from Ahn for Mortdh to appear at court arrived?

It had been a week since Navuh had dropped the warriors off at the most southern town along the coast of the middle sea. With plenty of money to exchange horses on the way, they should have covered the distance in six days.

Hopefully, nothing had happened to them on the way. Three elite immortal warriors were not easy to take down, but bands of bandits were known to take risks when the loot was tempting enough. The warriors might have flaunted their padded pockets in the towns they had stopped in on the way.

The guards standing outside Mortdh's tent bowed but refused him entry. "Lord Mortdh is not alone." One of them winked.

Even without the gesture, the sounds coming out from the tent were unmistakable.

There were at least two females in there, and judging by their throaty moans, both were enjoying themselves.

Navuh wondered whether they were harem girls that his father had brought with him from the several that he always had on hand, or had he summoned human priestesses from a nearby temple.

Mortdh's fertility temples were nothing more than glorified whorehouses, where any male could purchase sexual favors by offering tribute to Mortdh.

It was an excellent way to generate additional revenue without raising taxes. Mortdh had a knack for earning the admiration of his people despite taking away their rights and freedoms.

At first, the females were not too happy about the new laws, but humans had short memories. The new generation of girls, who had been born to Mortdh's reality, accepted it as the way it should be because they did not know anything else.

To pass the time, Navuh circled the encampment, shaking hands and talking to the soldiers. They admired and worshipped Mortdh, but they talked more freely with Navuh.

He wondered what would happen once Mortdh was gone. Would they worship him the way they worshiped his father?

Probably not. He was not a god.

The problem was, Navuh wanted to keep things more or less the way his father had set them up. Other than the breeding program, which Navuh was going to overhaul, everything else was working beautifully. The people were content and the taxes collected were plentiful.

Except, it was all hinged on Mortdh's worship. Without it, people might abandon his ideology as well. Unless Navuh could perpetuate it in his father's memory. Could an absent god inspire the same loyalty?

Time would tell.

When he returned, his father was finished and expecting him. "You can enter, Navuh," he called from inside the tent.

On his father's bed, two very young human women were sprawled, passed out from a venom-induced euphoria, their priestesses' robes sloppily draped over their naked bodies.

Navuh was surprised Mortdh had bothered to cover them at all. "Good evening, Father," he announced himself.

Stepping out from behind the partition, his bare chest glistening from the quick wash he had given himself, Mortdh grinned. "A very good evening indeed."

Evidently, the summons had not arrived yet.

"New priestesses?"

"Fresh, but not new. They were inducted four days ago. I wanted another taste and had them brought to me."

Inducting virgins into the fertility priesthood was one of the main reasons Mortdh loved touring his province so much. Each town had its own temple, and priestesses served only until they became pregnant, which meant a high turnover and a constant fresh supply of virgins.

Sacrificing her virginity to the god was every girl's dream, especially when combined with the hope of giving birth to a demigod son. Not that it had ever happened, but hope was a powerful thing.

Navuh bowed. "Would you like me to call in your servants to take the priestesses back to their temple?"

The things he and his father talked about required

privacy, and in order to cast a silencing shroud, the girls had to be removed from the tent first.

Mortdh waved a hand. "And have them bring dinner as well." He smirked. "Strenuous activity makes me hungry."

With a bow, Navuh turned on his heel and exited the tent. Outside, Mortdh's servants were clustered around a fire pit. The night was fast approaching and with it the mountain chill. In less than a moon cycle, it would start snowing.

"You two." Navuh pointed at the humans. "Get in the tent and carry out the priestesses."

The two jumped to their feet and rushed to do as they were told.

He pointed at the third one. "Bring the carriage around. The priestesses need to get back to the temple."

"Right away, my lord."

The fourth man was his father's personal valet—an immortal.

Navuh pointed at him. "Lord Mortdh wishes to dine."

The immortal bowed his head. "I will bring dinner expeditiously. Will you be dining with your father, Lord Navuh?"

"No, I will not." Later tonight, he was going to dine with Areana.

When Navuh reentered the tent, he found his father in a much different mood than the jovial one he had left him in.

Brows drawn tight, Mortdh was staring at his tablet.

The summons must have arrived.

The muscles in Navuh's body contracted painfully. Through sheer willpower, he loosened his body and painted a concerned expression on his face. "What is the matter, Father?"

Mortdh waved a hand, and the silencing shroud snapped into place with an audible pop. "I am summoned to appear before the council and stand trial for Khiann's murder."

Navuh widened his eyes. "But you did not do it!"

"It says here that three reliable eyewitnesses saw me kill him." He lifted his face and glared at Navuh. "The number three is not coincidental. Where are the warriors that went with me?"

"On leave in one of the coastal cities."

Mortdh kept glaring. "I doubt that. I bet they are at Ahn's court getting paid their weight in gold for providing false testimony to incriminate me."

Navuh felt faint with relief. Mortdh thought Ahn had concocted the accusation. "But how? I trust that you thralled them to forget the entire thing from start to finish, including their ride with you in the flyer?"

His compulsion was stronger than any thrall, but obviously, Mortdh could have not known that.

"I did. But Ahn is powerful. He could have restored their memories and then planted new ones to replace them."

Navuh shook his head. "I do not see how it makes sense. How would he know to pick up those three? And why? He could have picked any of our soldiers and planted the false memories in their heads."

Mortdh would have eventually asked himself the same questions, and then his suspicion would have turned to Navuh. By voicing them first, Navuh was hoping to deflect his father suspicion elsewhere.

"I am only assuming he has the three that were in on the plan from the start, but you might be right about them being any random soldiers." Mortdh started pacing. "I will tell you what happened. When the merchant could not be found by the princess when she came to visit him, Ahn realized that he had a perfect opportunity to frame me for his murder. But since he had no proof, the son of a diseased goat manufactured it."

"What are you going to do? Are you going to respond to the summons and argue your innocence?"

Mortdh eyed him with undisguised disdain. "You are supposed to be smart, Navuh. Why would I do that? He has three supposedly reliable witnesses. Nothing I can say would matter."

"So what now? I suggest you fly back to our stronghold immediately. We have some twenty soldiers who can block mind control. It is not enough to conquer the south, but it might be enough to defend you in case Ahn sends a delegation of gods to detain you."

In theory.

In reality, Navuh would ensure that their brains were wide open to invasion.

Besides, appearances were vitally important to Mortdh. He was not going to get up and run home to hide. It would make him look like a coward.

As Navuh had expected, his father waved a dismissive hand. "There is no rush. The big assembly will jabber for days before reaching a decision. And then weeks will pass before they get up here. I am going to respond to Ahn's summons by saying that I do not know what he is talking about and that the charges are manufactured, and then I am going to continue my tour as if nothing happened because nothing did."

Navuh affected a concerned expression. "I wish you would reconsider. Ahn might push for a quick conviction, and he might use his three airboats to transport the delegation. They might get here in days rather than weeks."

His father clapped him on the back. "You are a good son, Navuh, and I understand your concern for me. But I know Ahn, and I know the pompous bunch of gods who answer to him. They are incapable of reaching a quick decision and even less capable of implementing it." He clapped Navuh's back again.

50

ANNANI

*A*s Annani listened to the soldiers' testimony, her emotions ran from utter and complete despair to a hatred so hot and intense that it should have summoned bolts of lightning from the sky and incinerated Mortdh on the spot.

The need to avenge Khiann was the only thing keeping her from collapsing to the ground and waiting there until her body went into stasis from starvation.

If Mortdh were there, she would have clawed his eyes out with her bare fingers. Then, she would have punched a hole in his ribcage, pulled out his black heart, and stomped on it before letting the dogs eat what was left.

Hopefully, while he was still alive and aware.

Her hatred would have lent her the physical and mental strength needed to take down the powerful and evil god.

She should have done that the day that vile creature had come to persuade her to reconsider.

Khiann would have been alive if she had acted then.

Through the haze of pain, Annani was aware of how insane her thoughts were. They made her no better than that murderer. But Annani did not care. Any goodness she had possessed had died with Khiann. All that was left of her was a sack of misery and rage.

And guilt.

It was her fault. She should have never gone after Khiann and convinced him to mate her.

The savage brutality of the murder the soldiers had described made it painfully clear that she had grossly underestimated Mortdh's insanity and his hatred of her, and by association of Khiann.

She should have been more adamant and forbidden Khiann to go on the stupid caravan expedition.

She had not done enough to keep him home.

When the third soldier was finished repeating the testimony, Ahn rose to his feet and addressed the assembly. "We all have heard the damming testimony of these witnesses. I have personally verified that they are not lying. Since the accused is not here to defend himself, is there anyone who is willing to speak on behalf of Mortdh?"

The resounding silence was like music to Annani's ears. Glancing at Ekin and Toven, she saw that Mortdh's father and half-brother wore similar tight-lipped expressions. If they were not willing to speak on his behalf, no one else would.

Ahn waited a few more moments in case someone changed their minds, then continued. "Before we vote, I want to read to you Mortdh's response to the summons, even though I am under no obligation to do so. But as murdering a god is the gravest of offenses, I want to make sure that no one in the future could claim these proceedings were not fair."

There were a few murmurs, some agreeing with Ahn, and some that did not. Annani belonged to the second group. Who cared what the murderer had to say? If he denied it, no one would believe it. And if he was going to try and excuse his actions in any way, she did not want to hear it.

Ahn lifted his tablet. "I, the most exalted god Mortdh, did not kill the god Khiann. I will not honor the trumped-up charges against me by appearing at your sham of a trial and listening to the lies you have planted in the fake witnesses' minds. You can have your precious assembly of bobbing heads decide whatever they please, but I have no intention of showing up and submitting to your supposed justice. You are free to come to me, but unless it is to worship at my feet, you should come ready for war."

She now understood why her father wanted to read the murderer's response. If before hearing it some had still been undecided about Mortdh's guilt, they were firmly decided now.

Ahn put the tablet away and looked at his audience. "Raise your hand if you believe beyond a reasonable doubt that the god Mortdh is guilty of the murder of the god Khiann."

Annani raised her hand, as did each and every other god in the assembly chamber, which was all of them except for the murderer and her half-sister who was probably held captive by him. The soldiers who had accompanied her had not returned yet, so there was still a chance she had not reached Mortdh's stronghold. Annani hoped Areana had wised up and decided to run away and hide somewhere.

Otherwise, that evil hateful creature would probably do to her what he had done to Khiann.

Ahn was the last to raise his hand. "By a unanimous vote, the assembly of gods finds the god Mortdh guilty as charged."

51

AREANA

*A*reana knew something was wrong the moment Navuh entered the house. His angular features seemed even harsher than usual, his hollow cheeks hollower, his eyes deeply hooded but not with desire.

She could practically taste the dark energy rolling off him.

Without saying a word or even acknowledging anyone's presence aside from hers, he took her hand and pulled her toward her bedchamber.

What was he going to do to her when he got her alone?

Was he going to hurt her?

With a pang of regret, Areana realized that she did not trust him not to. By his own admission, Navuh was not a good man, and she feared discovering how bad was bad.

Sitting on her bed, he pulled her onto his lap, and with a sigh, closed his arms around her. His face buried in her chest, he seemed to be seeking solace.

"What is wrong?" She smoothed her hand over his silky hair, comforting him as she would a child.

"I have very grave news, Areana."

Her gut clenched painfully. "What is it?"

He took in a long breath. "There is no easy way to say this. Khiann is dead."

A shocking chill came over her as his words brought back an echo of a painful memory. "What do you mean Khiann is dead? How?"

Taking her hands, Navuh tried to rub the chill away. "I do not know. Ahn accused Mortdh of the murder, but Mortdh denied the allegation. It could have been bandits, and Ahn might have seized the opportunity to frame Mortdh."

"Poor Annani." Areana let the tears run free. "I wish I could go to her and comfort her, although I know nothing can. I would just hold her and let her cry."

"You cannot. Now more than ever it is important for you to stay hidden. Mortdh is enraged, and I do not know what he would do to you."

Fear made the lump already lodged in Areana's throat double in size. She could not breathe. Gasping, she squeezed Navuh's hand.

"Do not worry." He gently caressed her back. "As long as you stay hidden, you are safe here. I will not let anything happen to you."

The conviction in his voice and his warm hand on her cold back helped. The panic receded just enough for her to suck in a deep breath.

"For how long?"

"As long as it takes." He cupped the back of her neck and softly kissed her lips. "Mortdh was summoned to appear in front of the council, but of course he refused. It is likely that once sentencing is passed, Ahn will send a delegation of gods to arrest him."

A ray of hope made it into Areana's aching heart. "Will they sentence him to entombment?"

Navuh nodded. "I think so. From what I understood, the council was presented with extremely damming testimony from three reliable witnesses. There is no way to contest it."

Had she detected a smug note in Navuh's voice?

It occurred to her then that as Mortdh's second-in-command and official successor, Navuh would have known if his father had been planning to kill Khiann.

But that was neither here nor there.

Even if he had known about it, there was not much he could have done to prevent it. Navuh was a powerful immortal, but compared to Mortdh, his powers were insignificant.

"He will not go willingly. This will start a war," she whispered.

"Not necessarily." Again, there was a note of smugness in his tone. "Contrary to what we led everyone to believe, our army is not ready. We do not have enough warriors who can resist the gods' mind control."

He grimaced. "Mortdh fails to understand that it is hard to train soldiers against godly mind manipulation when the only god around who can test their mental blocks is him, and he is often too busy with other things. Bottom line, if Ahn sends a large enough delegation, they can overpower my father."

The implications were tremendous. With Mortdh out of the picture, Navuh would become the northern ruler, and she would happily join with him and rule by his side. Navuh was not like his father, and he would not keep her locked up in a harem. He would treat her with respect.

It would be the best possible outcome for her and for the future of their people.

Except, of course, for Khiann and Annani who had paid the ultimate price to bring about this unexpected outcome.

NAVUH

*L*ast night had been the first time Navuh had shared Areana's bed without making love to her. Instead, he had held her in his arms, and they had fallen asleep together.

When he had told her about Khiann's death, her glow had dimmed to such an extent that it had been as good as nonexistent. Navuh had feared that the troubling news had snuffed out the inner flame he had managed to rekindle. But as he had kept talking, and she had realized that Khiann's death might mean the end of Mortdh, some of Areana's glow had returned.

Evidently, the sweet and gentle goddess was not above being opportunistic. Still, for the sake of appearances, he had not initiated sex even though he had wanted her with every fiber of his being. Navuh had to pretend to be troubled by his father's actions, and Areana had been genuinely distraught over Khiann's death, probably because it brought back memories of her own loss.

As he entered Mortdh's tent, Navuh prepared to deliver more of his superb acting. Until his father was taken away,

Navuh would be giving some of the best performances of his life.

"Good evening, Father." He bowed. "Any news?"

Sitting on his throne-like chair, his chin propped on his hand, Mortdh pinned him with a hard stare. "Did Ahn's other daughter arrive yet?"

Navuh stiffened.

During the tour, he had visited his father nearly every day, and this was the first time Mortdh had asked him about Areana. "No. Would you like me to search for her? After our last talk concerning her, I assumed you could not care less whether she arrived or not."

Years of practice helped Navuh to control his body's instinctive responses to his father's intimidating glare. Hopefully, it was good enough to pass Mortdh's scrutiny.

"What do you think is taking her so long?"

Navuh waved a dismissive hand. "She is a spoiled goddess like all the others. When I visited her at the beginning of her journey, all she did was complain about how hard life on the road was. Then she whined about my refusal to take her in the flyer. She is probably stopping in every coastal town on the way and taking long rests in each one."

Mortdh nodded as if he had been expecting that exact explanation. "Most likely, she is doing it on her father's orders. I did a lot of thinking last night, and I came to the conclusion that Ahn has been planning this since the beginning. We thought we were playing him, when, in fact, he was playing us all along."

Navuh frowned. "I do not see how. He could have not anticipated the earthquake. None of this would be happening without Khiann really dying, or getting buried alive as is the case."

"True, and this is the only weak point in the scenario I

have pieced together. Although, it is possible that Ahn has a device that can cause earthquakes. Who knows what he brought with him from the home planet. But there is a simpler explanation. He might have been planning the same thing we did. Except, his motive was to frame me with the murder. I would not be surprised if there was a band of bandits hiding in the dunes and waiting for an opportunity to ambush the caravan."

Mortdh smoothed his hand over his beard and then shook his head. "I should have known it was a setup. The ruthless son of a diseased goat could not have cared less about his daughter's happiness. He would have never accepted the son of a merchant as her mate unless he was planning to get rid of him soon."

Navuh walked over to the table, poured wine into two goblets, and handed one to Mortdh. "Do you think he set her up with Khiann?"

After taking a long gulp of the wine, Mortdh put the goblet down. "I do not think so. The little tart had the hots for the young god, and Ahn saw an opportunity. He knew I would take offense, and he expected me to rage over it publicly. I played right into his hands. So when he staged Khiann's murder, everyone was ready to believe that I did it."

Thank the Fates for Mortdh's deep-seated hatred for Ahn.

As clever and as ruthless as Ahn was, he would have never gone as far as using his beloved daughter in such a scheme and causing her unimaginable grief.

If it were Areana, Navuh would have believed it, but not Annani.

"Maybe we can dig him out. Imagine Ahn's surprise when his supposedly dead son-in-law makes an appearance. I bet he did not account for this possibility in his elaborate scheme."

"Unfortunately, it is not feasible. I would not be able to find the exact location. We could dig for years and not find him."

53

ANNANI

*A*nnani held on as best she could until the voting was done and sentencing was passed.

Except, it had not brought her the satisfaction she had expected. She was consumed by grief, and the only thing she felt was pain. Death would have been welcomed, and she even spent a few moments thinking of how she could end her own life.

Regrettably, she could not behead herself or cut out her own heart. What she could do, though, was go into stasis. It was close enough to death to take away the pain. She would not feel anything.

But even that required another's help. Someone had to put the lid on her tomb, and no one was going to do that for her.

Perhaps she could ask Ekin to make her a tonic that would make her sleep indefinitely. Anything would be better than the horrific void in her heart. The agony was more than she could endure.

As through a long tunnel, she heard the gods' muted voices as they argued about how to detain Mortdh and bring him to justice. Some claimed he had a large army of immortals who were immune to the gods' mind control, while others argued that the rumors were greatly exaggerated and that a small delegation of gods would be enough to detain him.

Still others warned that upon hearing his sentence, Mortdh would go on the offensive and attack first, and that the gods should focus on shoring up their defenses.

"Come, Annani." Her mother wrapped her arm around her shoulders. "The voting is done, and there is no reason for you to stay and listen to them argue for days. None of what they are discussing requires the entire assembly to vote."

Leaning on Nai, Annani let her mother lead her away from the underground assembly chamber, up the stairs, and into her suite of rooms.

"Would you like me to stay with you tonight?" Nai asked as she covered Annani's trembling body with a thick blanket.

"Maybe just for a little while." Annani scooted sideways. "Would you lie next to me?"

Nai had never shared her bed with Annani. Maybe she had when Annani was a baby, but she could not remember it. They were not very close. But right now Annani desperately needed her mother's comfort.

"Of course." Nai kicked her sandals off and climbed in bed.

With her mother's arms holding her tight, Annani let out a shuddering breath. "What if he really launches an attack?"

"He will not."

"You cannot be sure of that. What if he does and we lose? I would rather die than let him capture me. In his hands, my fate would be worse than death."

"He is not going to attack, and he is never going to get you. You are depressed, which is entirely understandable, and this is why you gravitate toward the worst case scenarios. Your father knows what he is doing. Mortdh is going to end up exactly where he belongs, which is inside a sealed tomb."

"That is too merciful an end for him. I wish he would be thrown into shark-infested waters and torn to pieces."

Nai chuckled. "You are definitely your father's daughter. But sharks cannot harm a god. He would just take over their tiny brains and command them to carry him to shore."

"That is most unfortunate."

"Indeed."

Lying in her mother's arms and imagining more horrible endings for Mortdh made Annani feel a little better. Still, she was not so far gone that she did not realize that her mother could be wrong. Mortdh could be planning an attack already, and she was wasting her time fantasizing about revenge she could never have. Instead, she should be searching for a good place to hide.

As far as Annani was concerned, a hole in the ground would do. It was not as if she planned to keep on living without her Khiann.

But that was another fantasy.

A more realistic possibility was the far north. She had learned the language of the pale-skinned savages given to her by that evil creature. They had told her many stories about the place they had been stolen from. It was cold and snowy most of the year, and during those months there was no communication between the different tribes. In springtime, the snow melted, and that was when the festivities were held, and matings were arranged between the various tribes.

They lacked civilization up there in the frozen north, but she could bring it to them. After all, that was what gods did—they taught primitive humans how to live better.

To do that, however, she needed a set of instructions. Not a problem—everything she needed to know was stored on Ekin's tablet. She would have to steal it from him.

Except, Annani had no energy for any of it. Right now, the fantasy of crawling into a hole in the ground was what appealed to her the most.

Next to her, Nai stirred. "I am going to ask my maid to make us some of my special tea. It always helps me relax when I am emotionally disturbed." She dropped her feet over the side of the bed. "In the meantime, I suggest you wash your face and put on a nightgown. Your dress is wet."

It was. While listening to the trial, Annani had cried a river of tears. But until her mother had brought it up, she had not realized that her dress was soaked through.

"Let me help you up." Nai offered her hand. "Do you need my help changing clothes?"

"No, I can manage." Barely, but she refused to appear helpless.

"I will be back with the tea." Nai waited a moment longer, making sure Annani made it to the washroom.

The lethargy slowed her down, doubling or even tripling the time it would have typically taken her to wash and put on a fresh dress. She wished Gulan was there to help her. Things would have seemed a little less bleak with her friend by her side.

Why did the Fates hate her so much?

Was it because of her arrogance? Had she been too greedy?

Annani struggled mightily against the floor's pull. It

was so tempting to just let herself crumple and once more succumb to sobbing.

Except, her mother was coming back with the tea, and she did not want to appear so weak in front of Nai.

"A princess always keeps her chin up," her mother used to say. "It does not matter if a storm rages inside you or if you are bored or tired. The people derive solace from seeing their leader is strong and in control."

Sound advice, except Annani did not want to lead anyone. She wanted to shrivel away and die.

When she came out of the washroom, her mother was back, but she was not alone. Sitting with Nai and drinking tea was the blind soothsayer who Annani had hired to tell Gulan her fake fortune.

"As I have promised, I came to give you your foretelling, Princess Annani."

Waving a dismissive hand, Annani sat down and took the cup of aromatic tea Nai handed her. "You forget that I know your fortunes are fake."

The old human shook her head. "The fortune that you asked me to tell your maid was fake. But that was what you asked me to tell her. You paid me to do that, and I did. My own fortunes are not fake. What I see with my blind eyes comes to pass, and what I have for you is going to cheer your heart."

Annani doubted anything could do that. But she could humor the fortuneteller while drinking her mother's tea. Surprisingly, the herbal concoction was fast acting. Already, she could feel its calming effect.

"I am listening."

The human emptied her cup and put it down with a trembling hand.

"This is what the spirits whispered in my ears." She

cleared her throat and lifted her blind eyes up as if the prophecy was written on the ceiling.

"Do not despair, Princess Annani. Not all is lost. True love cannot die. Its fire cannot turn to ice. Your beloved's love floats in the ether ready to be reborn. Khiann will find a way to come back to you in some form. Seven children will be born to you, all different, but his spirit will shine through their eyes warm and bright. And one day, many years from now, he will come to you, and you will know him at first sight. I saw it all with my blind eyes, my lady, and everything I see with my second sight comes to pass."

It was a bunch of nonsense meant to cheer her up, but even though Annani knew that, it still made her feel a little better.

Or maybe it was the tea.

"Thank you. You have given me hope."

"My pleasure, Princess Annani." The woman leaned on her wooden staff and pushed up. "I will take my leave now."

"Wait, let me pay you." Annani rushed to retrieve her purse and pulled out a bunch of coins. "Thank you again."

The woman weighed the coins in her gnarled hand, smiled and bowed. "You are very generous, Princess Annani. May the Fates reward your generosity."

"The Fates hate me."

Lifting her hand, the fortuneteller pointed a finger at Annani as if she could see her. "You are mistaken, Princess Annani. The Fates are often harsh on their chosen, but they chose you for a reason. You are destined for greatness. One day, you will remember my words and know them to be true." With that, the woman shuffled out of the room.

"She is right, you know," Nai said. "Before you were born, a different fortuneteller told me the same thing."

Annani shook her head. "How can you be so naive?

They probably tell the same thing to every expectant mother. I am sure it doubles their tips."

Except, despite her skepticism, the soothsayer's words had managed to plant a seed of hope in her heart.

What if the old human had not made it up? What if one day Khiann's spirit was reborn and he would come looking for her? If she let Mortdh capture her, there would be nothing left of her for Khiann to find. Mortdh would torture her and lock her up in a dungeon for thousands of years. She would lose her mind long before Khiann's foretold rebirth.

And what about her supposedly great destiny? Surely it was not to become Mortdh's slave. Maybe it was to bring civilization to the north?

That would certainly qualify as a great destiny.

She had to run, even if for a little while, and the sooner the better. There was no point in delaying. She was going to load her airboat with the necessary supplies, as well as her seven Odus. Not only were they a gift from Khiann, but they were also indispensable for such an undertaking. The Odus were strong and could protect her, and she would not even have to feed them. They could survive on anything.

Up north, she could crawl into that hole in the ground she had been fantasizing about, and stay there for a few moon cycles. It did not really matter whether she mourned here or there.

She was leaving tonight.

Once her grief subsided some, she could either return home or stay up north and start working on that great destiny the two fortunetellers had prophesied for her.

It would depend on whether her father and the council of gods prevailed against Mortdh or the other way around.

54

NAVUH

*M*ortdh was back at the palace, which meant no more visits to Areana unless Navuh could come up with a convincing excuse for why he needed to borrow the flyer.

Another spying mission to the south?

A fake search for Areana?

Or maybe a search for the warriors that were supposed to be on leave?

But any of those suggestions might turn Mortdh's suspicions towards him. As long as his father believed that it had been all Ahn's doing, Navuh was safe.

Except, Ahn was taking his sweet time.

Mortdh had been right about the assembly deliberating endlessly and not reaching any conclusions as to how to detain him. In his usual arrogant manner, Mortdh had finished the tour as planned, not skipping over any town in his province—or rather over any of his fertility temples.

It was good news for Mortdh, but bad news for Navuh.

The longer it took Ahn to arrest Mortdh, the riskier the situation with Areana became. Mortdh might decide that he wanted to find her after all, and send Navuh to search for her, and then Navuh would have to come up with a good story why she could not be found.

The door opened, and his personal servant entered the reception chamber, then bowed. "As per your request, I am reminding you of the time, my lord."

"Yes, thank you." Navuh closed the ledger and pushed to his feet.

His father had demanded his presence at dinner, and the god did not tolerate tardiness.

"Greetings, Father." Navuh bowed and joined Mortdh at the table. "I just finished tallying this moon cycle's earnings, and I am happy to report that they are still increasing at a fast rate. This cycle was more profitable than the last by one-tenth. This is a very good growth rate."

Navuh had rushed the calculations so he could deliver the results and talk about something that had nothing to do with Ahn or the council. Increased profits always put Mortdh in a good mood.

"I am glad to hear that." Mortdh picked up his goblet. "Leave us!" he commanded the servants.

When they were alone, his father cast a silencing shroud and leaned back in his chair. "Imagine how fast our coffers will fill when we add the southern region's tax revenue." He took a long sip. "Tomorrow, I plan to put an end to this fiasco. It has gone far enough."

"How?"

An evil smile curled Mortdh's lips. "I will fly over and address the big assembly."

His father had finally lost his mind completely.

Good news for Navuh.

Except, it might be a ruse to gauge his response.

"I do not understand, Father. What are you hoping to

achieve by giving yourself up, leniency? They will detain you on the spot."

Mortdh lifted his goblet for Navuh to refill. "I do not think so. In his arrogance, Ahn failed to take into account that he might be held responsible for his criminal actions. Falsifying evidence to get rid of a competitor is not as grievous an offense as the murder of a god, but it is a crime nonetheless. I am going to force him to admit his lies and instruct the assembly to nullify the verdict and the resulting sentencing. Naturally, after his admission, Ahn will have to step down, and I will assume power."

"If I may ask, how are you going to achieve that?"

"It is all a question of power, my son. Who has more of it and is not afraid to use it. Ahn will have no choice but to admit what he has done."

It was official.

Anger and stress must have caused a dramatic escalation in Mortdh's insanity. He now believed himself to be more powerful than Ahn.

Except, Mortdh was not doing any of the things he usually did when in the grip of a psychotic episode. He was not raging, or spouting hateful words, or throwing things around. In fact, he appeared perfectly composed.

What if he had something up his sleeve?

It was a known fact that gods became more powerful as they aged, at least until they reached their full potential. Ahn was ancient, thousands of years older than Mortdh. Perhaps he had stopped increasing in power while Mortdh continued?

What if Mortdh could compel Ahn to tell the truth? Was that the secret weapon that he had been alluding to?

A cold chill ran down Navuh's spine.

If Mortdh was not completely insane, and he could

indeed force the truth out of Ahn, he would realize it had not been his uncle who had set him up, but his own son.

Navuh had to act fast.

Tonight, he was going to compel the flyer's maintenance crew to sabotage it so Mortdh would crash and burn before reaching Ahn's capital.

It was good that he had an alternative plan, and that he had prepared for it in case his elaborate and elegant one did not work out.

During Mortdh's tour, Navuh had taken the opportunity to chat with the flyer's mechanics and have them share a lot of technical information about its engine and what type of malfunction could cause it to explode. He had learned that it was sealed in an impenetrable compartment and that there was no way to cause it to malfunction.

The only way to make the flyer crash and burn was to place several timed explosives in strategic places. Fortunately, a large supply of those remained from the distant days of mining for gold and were still used for various building projects.

"I sense your anxiety, son, but you have nothing to worry about. I will emerge victorious."

"I cannot help but worry. I would not be doing my job if I did not advise caution."

"This is true. But sometimes taking risks is necessary."

55

NAVUH

The distance between Navuh's reception chamber and the flyer's hangar was precisely seven hundred and twenty-two paces long. The distance between the hangar and the landing pad was two hundred and fifteen.

It was the fourth time Navuh had counted them, and he was about to start the fifth.

Uncharacteristically, Mortdh had left early in the morning without his usual fanfare and without demanding that Navuh be there to see him off.

For some inexplicable reason, it bothered Navuh that he had not had the chance to say goodbye to his father. Mortdh was probably never coming back, which should make him glad, but all Navuh could feel was anxious energy swirling in his gut.

It was the uncertainty.

What if the flyer did not explode and Mortdh made it to Ahn's capital?

For all he knew, right now Mortdh could be sitting on Ahn's throne and planning Navuh's execution.

Perhaps he should go to his father's reception chamber and search for his tablet. Mortdh must have prepared a speech for his confrontation with Ahn, as well as his address to the council. It was likely that he had written it on his tablet first.

Except, after a thorough search of Mortdh's private quarters as well as his throne room and his reception chamber, Navuh had to conclude that his father had taken the tablet with him.

It was a shame. Navuh had hoped to inherit it along with all of his father's other possessions.

When three more hours had passed, and Mortdh still did not return, the tight knot in Navuh's gut started to ease.

His plan must have succeeded, and Mortdh was dead.

But until he got confirmation from his spies in Ahn's court, it was too early to celebrate. Regrettably, it would take several days for the news to arrive.

Two hours later, Navuh started smiling.

By nightfall, Navuh broke the seal on an old wine barrel, poured some into a decanter, and took it to his bedchamber to celebrate.

Mortdh was dead.

Otherwise, he would have already been back, swinging his sword to behead his traitorous son.

56

AREANA

"My lady." Tula stepped out into the garden. "A messenger from Lord Navuh has arrived, and he is waiting outside. The guards ask if it is all right to let him in the house."

Fear clenched Areana's heart. No one was supposed to know she was there. Navuh had told her to stay out of sight, and it was not likely for him to expose her whereabouts by sending a messenger. But what if something had happened and he needed to send her a warning?

If he was indeed the one who had sent the messenger, he would have also sent a note. Navuh was clever, he would have written something to let her know the note was really from him.

"Did he say anything about a note from Lord Navuh?"

"I will ask." The girl dashed away.

In the short span of time it had taken Tula to return, Areana's mind had managed to manufacture several catastrophic scenarios, starting with Mortdh finding out about her whereabouts and sending for her, to Navuh's untimely death at his father's hand.

"Lord Navuh sent a note." Tula handed Areana a rolled-up scroll. "It has his personal seal on it and everything. Two sickle swords crossed at the handle with the disk of eternity between them. What do you think it means?"

She could not care less. Breaking the seal without sparing it a glance, Areana unrolled the scroll.

Dear Lady Areana,

It is time for you to pack your things and continue your journey to its final destination. I wish I could have come and escorted you to the palace myself, but with my father gone, I am afraid I cannot leave court for an extended period of time. Regrettably, the flyer, which holds such fond memories for us both, is no longer available.

Lord Navuh.

After reading the short note two more times, Areana rerolled the scroll and tucked it inside her pocket. "Please ask the messenger if there is anything else he needs to tell me."

"Yes, my lady." Tula rushed out, once again forgetting to curtsey before leaving.

Except, did her young maid's less than perfect court manners still matter?

What did the note mean?

It was from Navuh, Areana knew that because of the reference to the fond memories from their time kissing and fondling in the flyer, but the rest was more ambiguous, and she was not sure what to make of it.

Navuh had visited her plenty of times while Mortdh was gone, but apparently he no longer had access to the flyer, which meant that Mortdh had taken it, or that it had malfunctioned and was no longer capable of flight.

Or both.

Had Navuh arranged for Mortdh to crash with the flyer?

It was the most likely explanation. Otherwise, Navuh would have not asked her to come.

Could she dare to hope?

Excitement bubbling in her chest, Areana pushed to her feet and called out, "Tula! It is time to pack our things."

NAVUH

*S*omething was terribly wrong.

Six days had passed since Mortdh had left, and still, there was no word from Navuh's spies in Ahn's court, or from any of the other informants scattered throughout the southern city-states.

At first, Navuh had come up with several plausible scenarios for why the network had gone quiet, but then disturbing rumors of a great calamity had started trickling in—of a deadly wind that had swept over the south, killing everything on its path.

People, animals, vegetation, everything was dying.

The flyer's crash probably had nothing to do with that, but the timing was too coincidental.

Navuh did not know much about the technology that propelled flyers, but according to its maintenance crew, the explosion had been supposed to be big enough to be seen from a league away, but not much farther than that. The plan was for it to occur just outside of the city walls, so it would be visible from Ahn's palace, but not cause too much damage.

Even if the technicians had miscalculated the distance, which was very possible, the explosion might have destroyed nearby structures and caused a fire, probably killing some, but it should not have caused a deadly wind to spread and kill every living thing it touched.

Suspicion and unease churning in his gut, Navuh turned to his servant. "Get the flyer's maintenance crew in here. I wish to question them."

"Right away, my lord."

While waiting for their arrival, Navuh did a quick sweep of his quarters, ensuring no one was milling around under this or that pretext, and then instructed the warriors stationed at the entry not to let in anyone other than the crew he had summoned.

His inner reception chamber was as soundproof as he could make it, but the talk he was going to have with the crew required the extra precaution.

When the four immortals arrived, he sent his servant away and locked the door for good measure.

"What can you tell me about the flyer's technology that you did not tell me before?"

The four exchanged puzzled glances.

"We follow the manual," the senior mechanic said. "The thing that powers the flyer is sealed inside a metal enclosure that is impenetrable, and we do not know what is inside. But the casing is so strong that it most likely survived the crash."

The man was not stupid and knew the reason for the questioning.

"Define most likely." Navuh pinned him with a hard stare.

"I am sure that it can be found intact. I do not know of a force that can break that kind of metal. It is not from this world."

It was from the home planet, where the flyer had been originally built. The explosion had been caused by other relics, albeit less mysterious and more abundant. Several small globs of explosive putty had been connected to an altitude gauge. Once the flyer descended to a low enough altitude, the gauge had been supposed to activate a chain of explosions.

None of that could cause a deadly wind.

The flyer was fueled by adding water to a container that fed it into the sealed compartment, so that could not have caused it either.

There was still another option.

What if Mortdh's secret weapon was indeed a real weapon and not an increase in his powers?

Navuh had never heard of a weapon capable of producing a deadly wind, but it could have been something the old gods had brought with them from their home-world.

"Do you remember anything out of the ordinary from the morning my father left?"

The immortals shook their heads.

A heavy weight settling in his gut, Navuh stared them down. "Do you remember anything at all?"

Their grimaces confirmed his suspicions. Trying to remember something which they had been thralled to forget was causing them headaches.

The question was whether he could override his father's thrall and compel them to remember. Hopefully, Mortdh had been sloppy and had not done it thoroughly. After all, as the only god in the stronghold, Mortdh had had no reason to suspect anyone of being able to undo his thrall.

Concentrating on the senior mechanic, who he knew was the most susceptible to compulsion, Navuh captured the man's gaze and pushed as much of it as he dared into his voice. Too much would fry the mechanic's brain, while too little might not be enough to override his father's thrall.

"I want to know everything Mortdh told you to do since he returned from his latest tour. I want dates and words and actions. Everything. Then I want you to tell me everything Mortdh did the morning he took the flyer."

As the man's eyes glazed over and drool started trickling from one corner of his mouth, Navuh thought he had gone too far and was ready to repeat the compulsion on the next one.

But then the senior mechanic started to talk. "Since Lord Mortdh returned from his latest tour, I saw him only twice. The night before he left, he called for me and told me to prepare the flyer for an early morning departure. I did as he asked, going through all the standard procedures. After that, we wiped the flyer clean until it shone, so Lord Mortdh could see his reflection in the metal. Then we pulled it out onto the landing pad."

Navuh chuckled. That sounded like his father. Mortdh had liked his toys and his women new and shiny, or at least looking like they were.

The chief mechanic continued. "Lord Mortdh arrived shortly thereafter, carrying his tablet under his arm and holding a long contraption in his other. I asked him what it was, and he said it was a secret weapon and winked. I asked what sort of a weapon? He answered it was a portable launcher and that it was capable of great destruction. Then he added that he hoped he would not have to fire it because threatening the assembly with annihilation should suffice. After that, he told us to forget we ever saw it, climbed into the cockpit, turned the engine on, and took off."

As the full picture started to take shape in Navuh's mind, a frosty chill seized his heart and then spread out to the rest of his body.

"That will be all. You may leave."

The men rose to their feet, bowed, and turned toward the door.

He stopped them before they reached it. "Just one more thing." He walked over and unlocked it, and then turned to face them. "You will remember everything about that morning—the portable launcher you saw in Lord Mortdh's hands, and all the things he said about firing it at the other gods. The only thing you will forget is the explosives you planted on his flyer."

Eyes glazed, the men bowed again and left.

Alone in his chamber, Navuh pulled out the decanter of old wine from the chest next to his desk and drank straight from the container.

Evidently, Mortdh had managed to fire the weapon before the flyer had exploded, killing everyone as he had plunged to his own death.

He must have taken the tablet with him in order to issue an ultimatum from a firing distance. Mortdh had intended to only threaten Ahn and the council with annihilation, but Ahn had probably dismissed it as empty threats and refused. Mortdh then flew into one of his rages and fired the weapon.

Navuh refused to even consider that the explosion might have caused the weapon to misfire because that would mean that he was responsible for wiping out most of the southern regions' population including all the gods.

Except for Areana.

As of six days ago, she was the only remaining goddess on earth, and she belonged to him.

Then it dawned on him. As of six days ago, he was the

most powerful male on earth. With the gods and everyone else in the south gone, Navuh and his army of immortals were the only superior people left.

He could rule the entire planet.

But then there was Areana.

The one remaining goddess.

The smart thing to do would be to get rid of her as well.

Except, he knew he could never bring himself to do that. Besides, Areana was such a weak goddess that she was of no consequence. He could pass her off as an immortal, lock her up in his harem, and compel all her servants to keep who she really was a secret.

It would be for her own protection.

A powerless goddess in a world ruled by immortals could become a target. Many had been wronged by the gods, especially by Mortdh. They would love nothing more than to take their vengeance out on a defenseless female.

Come to think of it, they might feel the same thing about him. Those who had been wronged by Mortdh might want to take revenge on Navuh, who they perceived as much less powerful than his father and therefore an easier target.

Let them try.

Navuh had an entire army of immortal warriors who were loyal to him. Now that there were no more gods, the need to train their minds against godly manipulation was gone too, and the warriors' time could be better spent.

On what?

Conquering the world, of course.

Giddy with the sense of power, Navuh laughed out loud.

The north and south were already his, which left the east and the west, where human civilizations were still in their infancy and ripe for the taking.

ANNANI

"*G*oddess." The chief hunter dropped to his knees in front of Annani. "I am Thaej, chief to clan Roga-rost, and I am of the deepest honor to receive you."

The other men followed his example.

Her arrival in a flying machine and her command of their language must have had led him and his tribesmen to believe that she was a real deity.

Annani was not about to correct their misconception.

She needed help from these humans.

It was so freezing cold. How these people survived in their icy wasteland was a mystery. She knew they were fishermen and hunters, but where did they find animals to hunt when she could see no vegetation?

Everything was buried under a thick layer of snow.

Forcing what she hoped was a reassuring smile, Annani put her hand on the top of his head and responded with the same wording the northerner had used. "I am the goddess Annani, and I am of the deepest honor to be received. I seek shelter among your people, and warm clothing if you can spare it."

If Thaej was surprised that a deity needed his help, as well as clothing to get warm, he did not show it.

"My people will be of the deepest honor to provide for you and your seven sacred warriors."

The Odus were impervious to the elements and did not need to cover themselves with furs. "My warriors were forged from special materials in the gods' realm. They feel neither chill nor heat."

The chief's eyes widened, and he bowed to the Odus. "Welcome to my clan, mighty warriors. My home is your home."

The chieftain was probably happy to get such formidable reinforcements. But if he thought to use them in skirmishes against other clans, he would be sorely disappointed. His countryman had told her about the endless bloody battles between clans. Unless his tribe was attacked first, she was not going to lend him her Odus.

Wrapping her arms around herself, Annani let out a frosty breath. Dressed in a tunic and a pair of pants suitable for the coldest days of the hot climate she had come from, she was barely able to control the shivers.

She was supposed to be a deity—an omnipotent creature. Then again, she could invent anything she wanted about what gods could and could not do. In fact, she could create a whole new mythology to suit her needs.

"The gods' realm is much warmer than yours, and I do prefer warmth."

The chief jumped to his feet. "My apologies, goddess." He removed the fur coat from his shoulders and offered it to her. "Would you accept this humble garment until a suitable one can be made for you?"

The thing stank, but Annani took it anyway. "Thank you. You are most generous."

The chief was a big human, and his coat was so long that it pooled around Annani's feet.

He glanced down at her inappropriate footwear. "You cannot walk to our caves in these, Goddess Annani. If you allow it, it would be of my deepest honor to carry you."

"Thank you for your kind offer, but only my warriors are allowed to touch my skin. It can be deadly to you." After inventing the first item in her new mythology, Annani turned to the Odus, who were standing behind her. "Okidu, you will carry me. The rest of you, please take the supplies out of the airboat and mark its location."

In a few hours, the aircraft was going to be entirely covered by snow. If she did not mark it, she would not be able to find it until the snow melted in the spring.

"Yes, mistress." The seven bowed in unison.

As Okidu lifted her into his arms, Annani tucked the long coat around herself, covering her feet and her hands. Unlike a human, she would not suffer from frostbite, but her extremities tingled painfully as her body pumped blood to the affected areas, rushing to repair the damage.

The chieftain waited for the Odus to unload the supplies. When they were done, he started walking. "Follow me."

With a sigh, Annani put her head on Okidu's chest and closed her eyes.

As a place to hide from Mortdh, she could not have chosen better, but in every other regard, she could not have chosen worse.

Bringing civilization to these people had been a naive notion. Their living conditions were too harsh to allow for anything other than basic survival. Civilization required spare time and resources that these people did not have.

But that was a worry for another day.

Just like these primitive people who were kindly offering her shelter, Annani could not spare the energy for grand undertakings. She needed all she had left in her just to survive.

Perhaps in time, when grief loosened its clawing grip on her heart, she could bring herself to hope again, and with it would come the strength to move forward.

But right now, all Annani wished for was a warm cave to hide in and a stack of thick furs to sleep on.

The end... for now.

Annani & Gulan's stories continue in
The Children of the Gods Series.

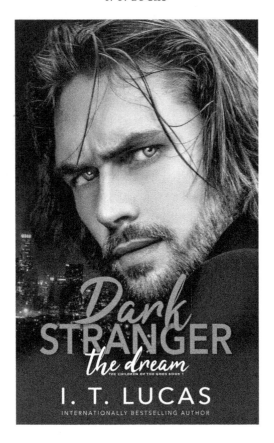

Dear reader,

Thank you for reading GODDESS'S HOPE.

As an independent author, I rely on your support to spread the word. So if you enjoyed the story, please share your experience, and if it isn't too much trouble, I would greatly appreciate a brief review on Amazon.

Click here to leave a review

Love & happy reading,

Isabell

To read an extended excerpt from
DARK STRANGER THE DREAM
Book 1 in the
THE CHILDREN OF THE GODS SERIES

JOIN
The Children Of The Gods
VIP Club at
itlucas.com
And get the access code to the VIP Portal

THE CHILDREN OF THE GODS SERIES

THE CHILDREN OF THE GODS ORIGINS

1: GODDESS'S CHOICE

When gods and immortals still ruled the ancient world, one young goddess risked everything for love.

2: GODDESS'S HOPE

Hungry for power and infatuated with the beautiful Areana, Navuh plots his father's demise. After all, by getting rid of the insane god he would be doing the world a favor. Except, when gods and immortals conspire against each other, humanity pays the price.

But things are not what they seem, and prophecies should not to be trusted...

THE CHILDREN OF THE GODS

1: DARK STRANGER THE DREAM

Syssi's paranormal foresight lands her a job at Dr. Amanda Dokani's neuroscience lab, but it fails to predict the thrilling yet terrifying turn her life will take. Syssi has no clue that her boss is an immortal who'll drag her into a secret, millennia-old battle over humanity's future. Nor does she realize that the professor's imposing brother is the mysterious stranger who's been starring in her dreams.

Since the dawn of human civilization, two warring factions of immortals—the descendants of the gods of old—have been secretly shaping its destiny. Leading the clandestine battle from his luxurious Los Angeles high-rise, Kian is surrounded by his clan, yet alone. Descending from a single goddess, clan members are forbidden to each other. And as the only other immortals are their hated enemies, Kian and his kin have been long resigned to a lonely existence of fleeting trysts with human partners. That is, until his sister makes a game-changing discovery—a mortal seeress who she believes is a dormant carrier of their genes. Ever the realist, Kian is skeptical and refuses Amanda's plea to attempt Syssi's activation. But when his enemies learn of the Dormant's existence, he's forced to rush her to the safety of his keep. Inexorably drawn to Syssi, Kian wrestles with his conscience as he is tempted to explore her budding interest in the darker shades of sensuality.

2: Dark Stranger Revealed

While sheltered in the clan's stronghold, Syssi is unaware that Kian and Amanda are not human, and neither are the supposedly religious fanatics that are after her. She feels a powerful connection to Kian, and as he introduces her to a world of pleasure she never dared imagine, his dominant sexuality is a revelation. Considering that she's completely out of her element, Syssi feels comfortable and safe letting go with him. That is, until she begins to suspect that all is not as it seems. Piecing the puzzle together, she draws a scary, yet wrong conclusion...

3: Dark Stranger Immortal

When Kian confesses his true nature, Syssi is not as much shocked by the revelation as she is wounded by what she perceives as his callous plans for her.

If she doesn't turn, he'll be forced to erase her memories and let her go. His family's safety demands secrecy – no one in the mortal world is allowed to know that immortals exist.

Resigned to the cruel reality that even if she stays on to never again leave the keep, she'll get old while Kian won't, Syssi is determined to enjoy what little time she has with him, one day at a time.

Can Kian let go of the mortal woman he loves? Will Syssi turn? And if she does, will she survive the dangerous transition?

4: Dark Enemy Taken

Dalhu can't believe his luck when he stumbles upon the beautiful immortal professor. Presented with a once in a lifetime opportunity to grab an immortal female for himself, he kidnaps her and runs. If he ever gets caught, either by her people or his, his life is forfeit. But for a chance of a loving mate and a family of his own, Dalhu is prepared to do everything in his power to win Amanda's heart, and that includes leaving the Doom brotherhood and his old life behind.

Amanda soon discovers that there is more to the handsome Doomer than his dark past and a hulking, sexy body. But succumbing to her enemy's seduction, or worse, developing feelings for a ruthless killer is out of the question. No man is worth life on the run, not even the one and only immortal male she could claim as her own...

Her clan and her research must come first...

5: DARK ENEMY CAPTIVE

When the rescue team returns with Amanda and the chained Dalhu to the keep, Amanda is not as thrilled to be back as she thought she'd be. Between Kian's contempt for her and Dalhu's imprisonment, Amanda's budding relationship with Dalhu seems doomed. Things start to look up when Annani offers her help, and together with Syssi they resolve to find a way for Amanda to be with Dalhu. But will she still want him when she realizes that he is responsible for her nephew's murder? Could she? Will she take the easy way out and choose Andrew instead?

6: DARK ENEMY REDEEMED

Amanda suspects that something fishy is going on onboard the Anna. But when her investigation of the peculiar all-female Russian crew fails to uncover anything other than more speculation, she decides it's time to stop playing detective and face her real problem—a man she shouldn't want but can't live without.

6.5: MY DARK AMAZON

When Michael and Kri fight off a gang of humans, Michael gets stabbed. The injury to his immortal body recovers fast, but the one to his ego takes longer, putting a strain on his relationship with Kri.

7: DARK WARRIOR MINE

When Andrew is forced to retire from active duty, he believes that all he has to look forward to is a boring desk job. His glory days in special ops are over. But as it turns out, his thrill ride has just begun. Andrew discovers not only that immortals exist and have been manipulating global affairs since antiquity, but that he and his sister are rare possessors of the immortal genes.

Problem is, Andrew might be too old to attempt the activation process. His sister, who is fourteen years his junior, barely made it through the transition, so the odds of him coming out of it alive, let alone immortal, are slim.

But fate may force his hand.

Helping a friend find his long-lost daughter, Andrew finds a woman who's worth taking the risk for. Nathalie might be a Dormant, but the only way to find out for sure requires fangs and venom.

8: Dark Warrior's Promise

Andrew and Nathalie's love flourishes, but the secrets they keep from each other taint their relationship with doubts and suspicions. In the meantime, Sebastian and his men are getting bolder, and the storm that's brewing will shift the balance of power in the millennia-old conflict between Annani's clan and its enemies.

9: Dark Warrior's Destiny

The new ghost in Nathalie's head remembers who he was in life, providing Andrew and her with indisputable proof that he is real and not a figment of her imagination.

Convinced that she is a Dormant, Andrew decides to go forward with his transition immediately after the rescue mission at the Doomers' HQ.

Fearing for his life, Nathalie pleads with him to reconsider. She'd rather spend the rest of her mortal days with Andrew than risk what they have for the fickle promise of immortality.

While the clan gets ready for battle, Carol gets help from an unlikely ally. Sebastian's second-in-command can no longer ignore the torment she suffers at the hands of his commander and offers to help her, but only if she agrees to his terms.

10: Dark Warrior's Legacy

Andrew's acclimation to his post-transition body isn't easy. His senses are sharper, he's bigger, stronger, and hungrier. Nathalie fears that the changes in the man she loves are more than physical. Measuring up to this new version of him is going to be a challenge.

Carol and Robert are disillusioned with each other. They are not destined mates, and love is not on the horizon. When Robert's three months are up, he might be left with nothing to show for his sacrifice.

Lana contacts Anandur with disturbing news; the yacht and its human cargo are in Mexico. Kian must find a way to apprehend Alex and rescue the women on board without causing an international incident.

11: Dark Guardian Found

What would you do if you stopped aging?

Eva runs. The ex-DEA agent doesn't know what caused her strange mutation, only that if discovered, she'll be dissected like a lab rat. What Eva doesn't know, though, is that she's a descendant of the gods, and that she is not alone. The man who rocked her world in one life-changing encounter over thirty years ago is an immortal as well.

To keep his people's existence secret, Bhathian was forced to turn his back on the only woman who ever captured his heart, but he's never forgotten and never stopped looking for her.

12: Dark Guardian Craved

Cautious after a lifetime of disappointments, Eva is mistrustful of Bhathian's professed feelings of love. She accepts him as a lover and a confidant but not as a life partner.

Jackson suspects that Tessa is his true love mate, but unless she overcomes her fears, he might never find out.

Carol gets an offer she can't refuse—a chance to prove that there is more to her than meets the eye. Robert believes she's about to commit a deadly mistake, but when he tries to dissuade her, she tells him to leave.

13: Dark Guardian's Mate

Prepare for the heart-warming culmination of Eva and Bhathian's story!

14: Dark Angel's Obsession

The cold and stoic warrior is an enigma even to those closest to him. His secrets are about to unravel...

15: Dark Angel's Seduction

Brundar is fighting a losing battle. Calypso is slowly chipping away his icy armor from the outside, while his need for her is melting it from the inside.

He can't allow it to happen. Calypso is a human with none of the Dormant indicators. There is no way he can keep her for more than a few weeks.

16: Dark Angel's Surrender

Get ready for the heart pounding conclusion to Brundar and Calypso's story.

Callie still couldn't wrap her head around it, nor could she summon even a smidgen of sorrow or regret. After all, she had some memories with him that weren't horrible. She should've felt something. But there was nothing, not even shock. Not even horror at what had transpired over the last couple of hours.

Maybe it was a typical response for survivors--feeling euphoric for the simple reason that they were alive. Especially when that survival was nothing short of miraculous.

Brundar's cold hand closed around hers, reminding her that they weren't out of the woods yet. Her injuries were superficial, and the most she had to worry about was some scarring. But, despite his and Anandur's reassurances, Brundar might never walk again.

If he ended up crippled because of her, she would never forgive herself for getting him involved in her crap.

"Are you okay, sweetling? Are you in pain?" Brundar asked.

Her injuries were nothing compared to his, and yet he was concerned about her. God, she loved this man. The thing was, if she told him that, he would run off, or crawl away as was the case.

Hey, maybe this was the perfect opportunity to spring it on him.

17: Dark Operative: A Shadow of Death

As a brilliant strategist and the only human entrusted with the secret of immortals' existence, Turner is both an asset and a liability to the clan. His request to attempt transition into immortality as an alternative to cancer treatments cannot be denied without risking the clan's exposure. On the other hand, approving it means risking his premature death. In both scenarios, the clan will lose a valuable ally.

When the decision is left to the clan's physician, Turner makes plans to manipulate her by taking advantage of her interest in him.

Will Bridget fall for the cold, calculated operative? Or will Turner fall into his own trap?

18: Dark Operative: A Glimmer of Hope

As Turner and Bridget's relationship deepens, living together seems like the right move, but to make it work both need to make concessions.

Bridget is realistic and keeps her expectations low. Turner could never be the truelove mate she yearns for, but he is as good as she's going to get. Other than his emotional limitations, he's perfect in every way.

Turner's hard shell is starting to show cracks. He wants immortality, he wants to be part of the clan, and he wants Bridget, but he doesn't want to cause her pain.

His options are either abandon his quest for immortality and give Bridget his few remaining decades, or abandon Bridget by going for the transition and most likely dying. His rational mind dictates that he chooses the former, but his gut pulls him toward the latter. Which one is he going to trust?

19: DARK OPERATIVE: THE DAWN OF LOVE

Get ready for the exciting finale of Bridget and Turner's story!

20: DARK SURVIVOR AWAKENED

This was a strange new world she had awakened to.

Her memory loss must have been catastrophic because almost nothing was familiar. The language was foreign to her, with only a few words bearing some similarity to the language she thought in. Still, a full moon cycle had passed since her awakening, and little by little she was gaining basic understanding of it--only a few words and phrases, but she was learning more each day.

A week or so ago, a little girl on the street had tugged on her mother's sleeve and pointed at her. "Look, Mama, Wonder Woman!"

The mother smiled apologetically, saying something in the language these people spoke, then scurried away with the child looking behind her shoulder and grinning.

When it happened again with another child on the same day, it was settled.

Wonder Woman must have been the name of someone important in this strange world she had awoken to, and since both times it had been said with a smile it must have been a good one.

Wonder had a nice ring to it.

She just wished she knew what it meant.

21: DARK SURVIVOR ECHOES OF LOVE

Wonder's journey continues in *Dark Survivor Echoes of Love*.

22: DARK SURVIVOR REUNITED

The exciting finale of Wonder and Anandur's story.

23: DARK WIDOW'S SECRET

Vivian and her daughter share a powerful telepathic connection, so when Ella can't be reached by conventional or psychic means, her mother fears the worst.

Help arrives from an unexpected source when Vivian gets a call from the young doctor she met at a psychic convention. Turns out Julian belongs to a private organization specializing in retrieving missing girls.

As Julian's clan mobilizes its considerable resources to rescue the daughter, Magnus is charged with keeping the gorgeous young mother safe.

Worry for Ella and the secrets Vivian and Magnus keep from each other should be enough to prevent the sparks of attraction from kindling a blaze of desire. Except, these pesky sparks have a mind of their own.

24: Dark Widow's Curse

A simple rescue operation turns into mission impossible when the Russian mafia gets involved. Bad things are supposed to come in threes, but in Vivian's case, it seems like there is no limit to bad luck. Her family and everyone who gets close to her is affected by her curse.

Will Magnus and his people prove her wrong?

25: Dark Widow's Blessing

The thrilling finale of the Dark Widow trilogy!

26: Dark Dream's Temptation

Julian has known Ella is the one for him from the moment he saw her picture, but when he finally frees her from captivity, she seems indifferent to him. Could he have been mistaken?

Ella's rescue should've ended that chapter in her life, but it seems like the road back to normalcy has just begun and it's full of obstacles. Between the pitying looks she gets and her mother's attempts to get her into therapy, Ella feels like she's typecast as a victim, when nothing could be further from the truth. She's a tough survivor, and she's going to prove it.

Strangely, the only one who seems to understand is Logan, who keeps popping up in her dreams. But then, he's a figment of her imagination—or is he?

27: Dark Dream's Unraveling

While trying to figure out a way around Logan's silencing

compulsion, Ella concocts an ambitious plan. What if instead of trying to keep him out of her dreams, she could pretend to like him and lure him into a trap?

Catching Navuh's son would be a major boon for the clan, as well as for Ella. She will have her revenge, turning the tables on another scumbag out to get her.

28: DARK DREAM'S TRAP

The trap is set, but who is the hunter and who is the prey? Find out in this heart-pounding conclusion to the *Dark Dream* trilogy.

29: DARK PRINCE'S ENIGMA

As the son of the most dangerous male on the planet, Lokan lives by three rules:

Don't trust a soul.

Don't show emotions.

And don't get attached.

Will one extraordinary woman make him break all three?

30: DARK PRINCE'S DILEMMA

Will Kian decide that the benefits of trusting Lokan outweigh the risks?

Will Lokan betray his father and brothers for the greater good of his people?

Are Carol and Lokan true-love mates, or is one of them playing the other?

So many questions, the path ahead is anything but clear.

31: DARK PRINCE'S AGENDA

While Turner and Kian work out the details of Areana's rescue plan, Carol and Lokan's tumultuous relationship hits another snag. Is it a sign of things to come?

32 : DARK QUEEN'S QUEST

A former beauty queen, a retired undercover agent, and a successful model, Mey is not the typical damsel in distress. But when her sister drops off the radar and then someone starts following her around, she panics.

Following a vague clue that Kalugal might be in New York, Kian sends a team headed by Yamanu to search for him.

As Mey and Yamanu's paths cross, he offers her his help and protection, but will that be all?

33: Dark Queen's Knight

As the only member of his clan with a godlike power over human minds, Yamanu has been shielding his people for centuries, but that power comes at a steep price. When Mey enters his life, he's faced with the most difficult choice.

The safety of his clan or a future with his fated mate.

34: Dark Queen's Army

As Mey anxiously waits for her transition to begin and for Yamanu to test whether his godlike powers are gone, the clan sets out to solve two mysteries:

Where is Jin, and is she there voluntarily?

Where is Kalugal, and what is he up to?

35: Dark Spy Conscripted

Jin possesses a unique paranormal ability. Just by touching someone, she can insert a mental hook into their psyche and tie a string of her consciousness to it, creating a tether. That doesn't make her a spy, though, not unless her talent is discovered by those seeking to exploit it.

36: Dark Spy's Mission

Jin's first spying mission is supposed to be easy. Walk into the club, touch Kalugal to tether her consciousness to him, and walk out.

Except, they should have known better.

For a FREE Audiobook, Preview chapters, And other

THE PERFECT MATCH SERIES

Perfect Match 1: Vampire's Consort

When Gabriel's company is ready to start beta testing, he invites his old crush to inspect its medical safety protocol.

Curious about the revolutionary technology of the *Perfect Match Virtual Fantasy-Fulfillment studios*, Brenna agrees.

Neither expects to end up partnering for its first fully immersive test run.

Perfect Match 2: King's Chosen

When Lisa's nutty friends get her a gift certificate to *Perfect Match Virtual Fantasy Studios*, she has no intentions of using it. But since the only way to get a refund is if no partner can be found for her, she makes sure to request a fantasy so girly and over the top that no sane guy will pick it up.

Except, someone does.

Warning: This fantasy contains a hot, domineering

crown prince, sweet insta-love, steamy love scenes painted with light shades of gray, a wedding, and a HEA in both the virtual and real worlds.

Intended for mature audience.

PERFECT MATCH 3: CAPTAIN'S CONQUEST

Working as a Starbucks barista, Alicia fends off flirting all day long, but none of the guys are as charming and sexy as Gregg. His frequent visits are the highlight of her day, but since he's never asked her out, she assumes he's taken. Besides, between a day job and a budding music career, she has no time to start a new relationship.

That is until Gregg makes her an offer she can't refuse —a gift certificate to the virtual fantasy fulfillment service everyone is talking about. As a huge Star Trek fan, Alicia has a perfect match in mind—the captain of the Starship Enterprise.

FOR EXCLUSIVE PEEKS

JOIN THE CHILDREN OF THE GODS VIP CLUB

AND GAIN ACCESS TO THE VIP PORTAL AT ITLUCAS.COM

CLICK HERE TO JOIN

(http://eepurl.com/blMTpD)

INCLUDED IN YOUR FREE MEMBERSHIP:

- **FREE** NARRATION OF GODDESS'S CHOICE—BOOK 1 IN THE CHILDREN OF THE GODS ORIGINS SERIES.
- PREVIEW CHAPTERS.
- AND OTHER EXCLUSIVE CONTENT OFFERED ONLY TO MY VIPS.

Made in the USA
Monee, IL
21 March 2022